MARVELOUS
MARVIN

and the

Pioneer
Ghost

MARVELOUS MARVIN

MARVIN

and the

Pioneer Ghost

Bonnie Pryor

illustrated by

Melissa Sweet

Morrow Junior Books   New York

Monotype with mixed media were used for the illustrations.
The text type is 13-point Carmina Light/Bitstream.

Library of Congress Cataloging-in-Publication Data
Pryor, Bonnie.
Marvelous Marvin and the pioneer ghost/Bonnie Pryor;
illustrated by Melissa Sweet.   p.   cm.
Summary: Marvin enlists the help of his twin sister, Sarah, and
Ernie, the biggest boy in the fourth grade, to solve a mystery
involving a ghostly figure and the polluting of his favorite stream.
ISBN 0-688-13886-1
[1. Mystery and detective stories.   2. Ghosts—Fiction.   3. Brothers
and sisters—Fiction.]   I. Sweet, Melissa, ill.   II. Title.
PZ7.P94965Mam 1995   [Fic]—dc20   94-33237   CIP   AC

To Bob—
who is pretty marvelous also
—B.P.

To Larry and Tracy
—M.S.

CONTENTS

MARVELOUS
MARVIN
and the
Pioneer
Ghost

ONE

A Mysterious SIGHTING

Marvin Fremont sprawled in a chair in his room, thumbing through a book of ghost stories he'd just checked out of the library. His chair was turned so that he could prop his bare feet on his windowsill. It was a Sunday afternoon in April, and a long week of spring vacation stretched ahead. Even better, unlike other spring vacations that had been snowy and cold, this year the weather was almost summery. Marvin was all set to enjoy a relaxing hour in the sun.

His twin sister, Sarah, who hardly ever sat still, and certainly not for a whole hour, burst into his room. "Marvin!" she yelled.

When there was no answer, Sarah bent over the chair. "Marvin," she repeated.

Annoyed, Marvin held his place with his fingers and shut the book. "What?"

"Mom said my karate class could meet at the house," Sarah said, flopping herself down on Marvin's bed. Noticing that her brother looked alarmed, she laughed. "Not for practice, silly. We are going to talk about ways to earn money for the trip to the state championships. But it is a great time for you to meet everyone."

"No thanks," Marvin said. "I've got some things to do."

Sarah frowned. "Like what?"

"Like read my book," Marvin said firmly. He casually turned the book so the title was hidden. He was sure Sarah would scoff at the idea of ghosts.

Sarah noticed that he was hiding the title. Since Marvin had been reading a lot of detective stories the past few months, she was certain that was what he was reading now. Marvin and his sister had helped catch a gang of car thieves the previous fall, and she knew he was hoping to find another crime to solve. "Jeepers, Marvin," she said reasonably. "I don't think there are very many crooks living in Liberty Corners. But if you really do want to be a detective, I'd think you'd be interested in anything that would help you defend yourself."

"We managed to solve one mystery without a lot of self-defense," Marvin said. "Sherlock Holmes didn't do karate," he added with a wave at his shelfful of mystery books. "He solved all his mysteries with his brain."

Sarah threw up her hands in surrender. "I have to get ready. Everyone will be here any minute," she said as she hurried out the door.

Marvin slipped on his socks and shoes and a light jacket. Picking up his book, he headed for the front door. Outside, the late-afternoon sun glared into Marvin's eyes, briefly blinding him. He took two steps and ran smack into Mean Ernie Farrow, who was just heading in the door.

"Whoa, watch out, little buddy," Ernie's voice boomed. He grabbed Marvin and steadied him before he could fall. Embarrassed, Marvin thanked him.

"Hey, I thought you'd be at this meeting," Ernie said. "I just joined."

Several members of the karate class knocked at the door, sneaking looks at Ernie. Marvin knew they must look strange together. Most of the kids were afraid of Ernie, who was the biggest boy in the fourth grade. He towered at least a head over Marvin. But ever since Ernie had helped Marvin solve the mystery of the stolen cars, he'd insisted he was Marvin's protector.

"I've got something to do," Marvin explained feebly.

Ernie grinned and flexed his muscles. "Don't you worry about a thing. When I learn karate, I'll be able to protect you from anybody."

"I don't need—," Marvin began, but Ernie waved and barged in the door without listening.

Marvin climbed on his bike and pedaled slowly onto Elm Street. Today, instead of heading toward the small shopping center a few blocks up the street, Marvin turned in the other direction, to where Elm Street ended at Creek Road. The road curved, following the twists and turns of Liberty Creek. Here the houses were farther apart and there were fewer cars to worry about.

After a few minutes Marvin got off his bike and pushed it behind several large boulders. Then he walked down a little path through the woods. Marvin often came to this spot. Even though it was only a short distance from his house, it felt like another world. Soon he could hear the gurgling rush of water as Liberty Creek tumbled over its rocky creek bottom. The creek was fairly wide at this point but not very deep. In most places it came up only to Marvin's knees. Liberty Creek meandered through this neighborhood, finally flowing into the river a few miles downstream.

Marvin settled down by the stream bank, with his back leaning against the gnarled roots of a sycamore tree. The ground felt damp. After a moment he took off his jacket and spread it on the ground to sit on. For a while he was lost in his book. It was pleasantly warm, too early in the spring for many bugs but with just enough new green leaves to filter the sun. Marvin rested his head back and closed his eyes. Before he knew it, he had drifted off to sleep.

Sometime later Marvin's head jerked up and his eyes flew open. For a second he was confused, trying to remember where he was. He shivered and reached to close his jacket. Then he remembered he was sitting on it. It had been warm when he fell asleep, but now the air seemed icy. He tried to figure out how long he had slept. The sun was nearly gone, with only a few rays that gave a pink tint to the horizon. It must be close to eight o'clock, he thought with alarm. His parents would be worried. Uneasily, Marvin looked around. Why did he feel as though he was being watched? The woods seemed unnaturally still, without even a breath of wind. A prickly feeling ran down Marvin's spine.

"W-who's there?" Marvin asked out loud, unhappy that his voice trembled.

When no one answered, he spoke again, trying to make his voice stern. "Is someone here?"

A sound—perhaps a breeze moaning through the trees, perhaps something more sinister—made him glance downstream.

Marvin's breath caught in his throat. There was a man about a hundred feet away, half hidden by the shadowy trees. His clothes were ragged and appeared old-fashioned. A white mist curled around the man's legs. It made it seem as if the man drifted above the mist or perhaps was a part of the mist. The mist swirled, concealing the man. Suddenly Marvin wasn't sure he'd really seen someone. Perhaps it was just a trick of the creeping dark and the mist. Marvin rubbed his eyes, trying to see. He felt frozen in place, as though his arms and legs had lost the strength to move. Shakily he reached for his jacket and book, intending to grab them and run. He forced himself to look back. Only a faint trail of mist marked the spot.

TWO

Ernie's
PLAN

Early Monday morning, before their parents were up and getting ready for work, Sarah burst into Marvin's room and bounced on his bed. "Okay, what's going on?" she demanded.

"What do you mean?" Marvin asked innocently.

"You came running in the house last night, after dark, your face as white as a sheet. Then you told Mom and Dad some silly story about being late because the chain came off your bike."

"How do you know that wasn't true?" Marvin asked, stalling for time while he decided how much to tell her.

"You're not the only one who can be a good detective," Sarah said with a smirk. "If you'd been fixing your chain, you would have had grease on your hands. I just didn't say anything last night because Mom and Dad were there."

"I was late because I fell asleep by Liberty Creek," Marvin reluctantly admitted. "But when I woke up, I saw something really weird." Seeing Sarah's look, he told her the whole story.

Suddenly Sarah jumped up and started rummaging through his stacks of comic books.

"What are you doing?" Marvin asked.

"Okay." Sarah chuckled. "Where is it?"

"Where is what?"

"The comic book you're reading," Sarah said. "The one about *ghosts.*"

"I don't have a comic book about ghosts," Marvin said, sounding indignant.

Sarah spied his library book. "Aha!" she said triumphantly. "I knew it."

"All right. I admit I have been reading about ghosts. But I really did see one. At least I think I did."

"Oh, come on, Marvin. There is no such thing as ghosts. And even if there were, why would one be standing by Liberty Creek? You admitted you were asleep. You probably only dreamed it."

"I had been asleep," Marvin explained patiently. "I was awake when I saw the ghost, though."

"Maybe it was just some guy out for a walk, and you scared him as much as he scared you."

Marvin shook his head. "It's hard to explain. But I know it was a ghost."

"Did you tell Mom and Dad?" Sarah asked.

"They'd just say I have too much imagination." Marvin sighed. He opened his desk and took out a small notebook.

"Why *would* a ghost be standing by Liberty Creek?" he mused. "I'm going back to the spot where I saw it and look for clues."

"I'll come with you," Sarah said.

"I thought you didn't believe me," Marvin said.

Sarah grinned at him. "I don't. But you might need some help if that guy comes back and grabs you." She made a karate chop in the air.

After a hasty breakfast, Marvin scribbled a note to their parents saying they were going for a bike ride.

"Wait a minute," Sarah said. She dashed upstairs to her room and returned with her camera. "Maybe I can get a picture of this ghost," she said teasingly.

As they pushed their bikes out of the garage, Mr. Wolfe, their next-door neighbor, waved at the twins and gave them a rather toothy grin. He was busy hanging a new bat house on a pole. Marvin and Sarah liked Mr. Wolfe, although there was something about him that always made Marvin shiver. The twins returned the wave as they headed down the street.

Nothing about the woods seemed ominous today. The early spring sun was still unusually warm, and the trees were full of birds busily building places to raise their young. The woods seemed so alive that Marvin began to doubt what he had seen. Yet, as they reached the old sycamore tree, something seemed different. Were the woods just a little darker here? Even Sarah seemed to feel the change. "I wish I'd brought my sweater," she said. Glancing around nervously, she walked a bit closer to Marvin.

A wisp of fog still wavered over the grass where Marvin thought he had seen the ghost. Marvin pointed. "This ground is damp enough to show footprints. But I don't see any." He knelt and checked the ground through his magnifying glass.

"I'm sure this is where the ghost stood," Marvin said. He pointed to a patch of wild violets near the tree. "None of these flowers seems crushed. That proves it was a ghost."

"Maybe you are wrong about where he was standing," Sarah said as she poked around, looking for tracks. "Or as I said before, you dreamed it."

"I was awake," Marvin said, sounding irritated.

Sarah looked unconvinced. "This seems like a pretty dumb place for a ghost to hang around. Shouldn't he be haunting old houses or something?"

"This book I read once said ghosts stay in a place because they have unfinished business there," Marvin said.

"Shh." Sarah held her finger over her mouth. They both froze at the sound of someone walking through the woods.

"Quick, let's hide," Marvin whispered. He pulled Sarah behind a tree as the crunch of leaves and snapping twigs got closer.

"That's an awfully noisy ghost," Sarah whispered.

Marvin groaned. "It's worse than a ghost." Peeking out from behind the tree, he watched as someone stepped into the clearing, picked up some stones, and tried skipping them across the stream.

"Ernie Farrow," Sarah said out loud.

Ernie whirled around and saw them. For a second he seemed startled. Then his face broke into a wide grin. "It's my little buddies! What are you two doing here?"

"Just taking a walk," Marvin said quickly. He looked around. Sunlight streamed through the trees. The fog had disappeared and the woods seemed perfectly normal.

Ernie made a pretend karate chop in the air. "You really should take karate lessons. In case we find any more crooks."

Marvin just shook his head.

"I've been waiting all winter," Ernie complained. "I thought when everyone heard how we captured those crooks, someone would ask us to solve another mystery."

"Marvin *has* found a little mystery," Sarah said slyly, ignoring Marvin's glance. "He thinks he saw a ghost last night."

Ernie's grin was nearly as wide as his face. "Don't you worry, little buddy. I'll protect you from those big bad ghosts."

Marvin turned away, but Ernie reached out and held his arm. "Don't get mad. I was only teasing. Tell me about it."

Reluctantly Marvin told his story again.

"It's spooky that time of day," Ernie said. "Sometimes I get a little nervous myself.

Maybe it was just a man out fishing or something."

Marvin shrugged. As he stood by the stream in bright daylight, the thought of a ghost did seem foolish.

"Hey," Ernie said suddenly. "I've got a great idea. Remember that detective agency we were going to start last fall? Why don't we make a clubhouse and have the agency there?"

"That new teen center near our house would be a perfect place to meet," Sarah said, sounding interested. "But I heard that no one under twelve can go."

"Well, it is a teen center," Marvin said reasonably.

"Anyway, that's not private enough," Ernie said. "I like my idea better." He snapped his fingers. "I've got an old tent. We could use it until we think of something better. Come on over to my house and we'll set it up. I live just over there." Ernie pointed to a small house barely visible through the trees.

"That sounds like a dumb idea," Marvin said without thinking. "A detective agency in a tent?"

Ernie's face darkened. "I thought you two were my friends."

Sarah nodded and smiled. "We are," she said. "And your idea about the tent is too a good one. As a matter of fact, it's one of the best ideas I've ever heard."

THREE

Mr. Dinkerhoff's FACTORY

Ernie led the way through the woods to his house. Marvin pulled Sarah's arm until they lagged a few steps behind. "I can't believe you want to help Ernie set up an old tent for a clubhouse," he whispered.

"In the first place," Sarah whispered back, "I feel a lot safer having Ernie for a friend than an enemy. And besides, I figure that once the tent is up, it will probably occur to Ernie to ask us to camp out. Think about it. Ghosts come out at night. Mom and Dad would never let us go into the woods at night, so there is no real chance to investigate. But they might let us go camping at Ernie's house, which just happens to be right near where you say you saw the ghost."

Marvin nodded. "Pretty good thinking. Unless of course I really did see a ghost. Then camping where one might be is pretty dumb."

"Come on," Ernie urged, waiting for them to catch up. They left the woods and crossed a small unmowed yard dotted with bright yellow blooms. Ernie looked embarrassed. "Our lawn mower's broken," he said.

"I like dandelions," Sarah said.

Ernie gave her a sharp look, as if he thought she was secretly making fun.

"I like them, too," Marvin said. He picked a puffy head and blew. Tiny white seeds parachuted across the grass.

Ernie climbed the steps to a cluttered porch. "The tent is right here. But I want to show you something neat that I did this morning. I got the idea from one of those detective magazines you lent me. You'd better stay out here, though. My mom works in a factory at night. I think she's still asleep."

The twins sat on the wooden porch steps to wait. A second later Ernie opened the sagging screen door. He was holding a blank piece of paper, which he handed to Marvin. "I wrote a message in invisible ink."

Marvin bent to sniff the invisible ink. "Lemon juice!" he exclaimed.

Ernie nodded, looking disappointed that Marvin had figured out his secret so easily. "If you hold it near a lightbulb, it turns a little bit brown and you can see the writing. We could write messages to each other in school. If Mrs. Pfeiffer sees it, she will just think we're passing a plain piece of paper."

"Only one problem," Marvin said. "If you are in school, where are you going to get the lemon juice?"

"Or the lightbulb," added Sarah.

Seeing Ernie's unhappy face, Marvin said quickly, "It might come in handy sometime when we're solving a mystery."

Ernie looked pleased. "Mom gave me a chemistry set for my birthday. It's *great*. I'll bet I can make all kinds of stuff that will help us catch criminals. You know, it's too bad we can't use the storage building in back of that empty house up the road for a clubhouse. It would have been perfect. But someone's moving in. I saw the moving van yesterday."

"What are we going to do in this club?" Marvin asked. "Besides solve mysteries."

"Well, we can catch ghosts," Ernie said with a grin. He rummaged through a jumble of things stacked on his porch and tugged out a long pole from under some boxes. "We could even go fishing."

The three detectives agreed to set up the

tent in a pretty little clearing between the creek and Ernie's house. Then the twins helped Ernie pile the tent and the fishing poles on the ground at the bottom of the steps. Before they could carry the supplies to the clearing, however, Mrs. Farrow appeared at the door and told Ernie to come up. She was wearing a bathrobe, and she looked sleepy. After a minute of conversation, Ernie returned to the yard, where the twins were waiting. He was frowning.

"Is your mom upset that we woke her up?" Marvin asked.

Ernie shook his head. "Mom is buying a new television on layaway from Mr. Snyder at the appliance store. She has to make a payment on it. But our car is being fixed at the garage. Mom wants me to walk over to Snyder's and pay it for her."

"We'll walk with you," Marvin offered.

"We can take the shortcut," Ernie said as they started out. He pointed to a faint trail leading through a wooded area. "It comes out behind that old factory. Then we can cut across the highway to the appliance store."

Ernie marched ahead, clearly unhappy about his errand. Marvin didn't mind the walk at all. It felt good to be out in the sunshine, and for a few minutes he and Sarah followed Ernie, not talking, simply enjoying the day. After a while they left the woods and walked through a field behind a small dilapidated brick factory building set back from the highway.

As soon as they reached the factory's parking lot, their way was blocked by a scowling man with a fringe of dark hair framing his bald head. He shook the broom he was holding like a weapon. "You kids don't belong here," he snarled.

Ernie gulped. "We were just taking a shortcut to the appliance store," he said meekly.

"Next time use the road," the man growled. He continued to glare suspiciously at them as they hurried past the building.

Two men were loading boxes into a small delivery truck parked at a loading dock. Mr. Dinkerhoff, the factory owner, was standing outside the door, talking to a younger man.

"The new machine could do the work of twenty people in half the time," Marvin heard the young man say.

"But then all my workers would be out of a job," Mr. Dinkerhoff answered. "Most of my people have been here for years."

"They're going to be out of work anyway if you don't modernize," the younger man said. "Times have changed. There's hardly a market anymore for the things you sell."

The scowling man walked over and spoke to Mr. Dinkerhoff in a low voice. Mr. Dinkerhoff looked up and gave the children a friendly wave. "It's all right, Alfred. These children are friends of mine.

"I hope Alfred didn't scare you," Mr. Dinkerhoff continued. "We've had some things missing, and Alfred is just trying to help."

"He did scare us a little," Sarah said, with an accusing glare over her shoulder at Alfred.

"Sorry," he mumbled, not sounding sincere. He moved off with his broom, vigorously sweeping but still watching them with suspicious eyes.

"Alfred's been with me a long time," Mr. Dinkerhoff said. "He thinks it's his job to watch over me."

Sarah smiled at Mr. Dinkerhoff. Even though many adults in the community, including Mr. and Mrs. Fremont, complained that the Dinkerhoff factory was an eyesore and should be torn down, Marvin and Sarah thought Mr. Dinkerhoff was one of the nicest people in town. Every year he sponsored a girls' softball team. Last summer Sarah had worn the uniform with DINKERHOFF NOVELTIES written in red across the back. Mr. Dinkerhoff had showed up at every game to cheer them on.

Mr. Dinkerhoff's mouth was almost hidden by his long, bushy mustache. "This is the girl who won the tournament for our team last summer," he said to the younger man, who was looking impatient.

Sarah blushed. "It was just a lucky catch."

Mr. Dinkerhoff chuckled. "The bases were loaded. The other team had two outs, but then their best hitter came up to the plate." He acted out the story, swinging an imaginary bat. "Crack!" he yelled. "The ball headed straight for the pitcher's mound. Well, this young lady jumped up about ten feet in the air and caught that ball just as easy as you please."

Ernie looked at Sarah admiringly. "I didn't know that."

"She had her picture in the paper," Marvin said proudly.

"Oh, by the way, this is my nephew, Roger Klinger," said Mr. Dinkerhoff. "He's come to help me run my factory."

"Not that he listens to anything I say," said the younger man. He smiled. "I'd better get back to work."

Mr. Dinkerhoff watched his nephew walk inside the factory. "Let me show you my latest creations," he said, "but don't tell my nephew. He thinks we should keep them a secret so no one can copy them. You are the first to have a look." Reaching into his bulging pockets, he pulled out a handful of plastic finger puppets. There were Christmas trees with little arms, Santas, and even some reindeer with packages on their antlers. They each jiggled merrily when he put them on his fingers. "What do you think?"

"They're cute," Sarah said. "It's a long time until Christmas, though."

"We have to make them in the spring so they will be ready for the holidays," Mr. Dinkerhoff explained. "Stores and catalogs will start ordering now. My nephew wants to change all our equipment to make boring things like parts for appliances and cars. He says we would make a lot more money that way." Mr. Dinkerhoff sighed. "I suppose he's right. But these are much more fun, don't you agree?"

"Mr. Dinkerhoff makes all kinds of plastic novelties," Sarah explained to Ernie.

Ernie fitted the puppets on his fingertips and wiggled them. "These are neat," he said.

Marvin noticed Mr. Snyder standing at the open door of his appliance store. He was staring across the street at Mr. Dinkerhoff's factory. It reminded Marvin of their errand. They said good-bye to Mr. Dinkerhoff and waited at the stoplight until the traffic was clear to cross the highway. By that time a customer had arrived, and Mr. Snyder had disappeared inside his store.

Ernie ran his hand admiringly over the hood of a shiny new black sports car. "I think this is Mr. Snyder's car. It was parked here when Mom bought the TV. I'm going to have a car like this when I grow up."

"He probably doesn't like anyone touching it," Marvin said. Ernie shrugged and gave the car a last yearning look as they entered the store.

Mr. Snyder was at the back, explaining the features of a new refrigerator to a customer. They wandered around the television department until Mr. Snyder was finished. It was interesting to see twenty televisions, all showing the same program.

"May I help you?" Mr. Snyder was a tall thin man, balding on top. Even standing still, he looked rushed. He drummed his fingertips on the counter while Ernie explained his errand and gave Mr. Snyder an envelope from his mother.

"Oh yes," Mr. Snyder said, writing out a receipt. "I saw you kids across the street. You shouldn't play around Dinkerhoff's factory. No telling what kinds of junk or dangerous chemicals are there."

"We were just talking to Mr. Dinkerhoff," Sarah explained, sounding defensive. "He's really nice."

Mr. Snyder shrugged. "He is a pleasant enough person, I suppose. Nevertheless, I can tell you all of us businesspeople wish he would fix up that old place." Mr. Snyder sighed. "I suppose he can't afford to. He probably doesn't make much money from those little finger toys."

Marvin looked surprised. "How did you know about the finger puppets?"

A young couple entered the store and began to study the televisions. "Mr. Dinkerhoff showed them to me the other day," Mr. Snyder answered as he hurried away to help his customers.

FOUR

An UNPLEASANT DISCOVERY

Aware that Alfred might be watching, Marvin, Sarah, and Ernie crossed the highway and walked past the factory to the corner of Creek Road. On the other side of the factory, Liberty Creek flowed under the highway bridge, but Creek Road ended there.

"I wonder why Mr. Dinkerhoff said we were the first to see his finger puppets," Marvin said.

"Maybe he just forgot he had showed them to Mr. Snyder." Sarah shrugged.

"Hey," Ernie said. "Who is that?" They had reached a large two-story house that was much grander than most of the homes on Creek Road. It had stood empty for over a year. Now, a tall man was painting something on the mailbox. A slender girl about the same age as Marvin and Sarah stood watching.

"That must be the new people. You said you saw a moving van," Sarah remarked quietly. She glanced admiringly at the house.

A curving driveway cut through the beautiful front yard, which had been maintained while the house was up for sale. Behind the house was a patch of woods, and beyond that was the creek.

The man noticed them watching and smiled. The girl studied them quietly. "My daughter thinks my letters are crooked," he said, stepping back and studying his work. "See what you think."

The name CROSS was lettered on the mailbox. "I think the s's go up a little," Sarah said. "I'll bet you could fix it if you made the bottom of the s's a bit wider."

The man slowly widened the bases of the letters and stood back again.

"Perfect," said the girl, speaking at last.

"Perfect for our first mailbox," the man said.

The girl looked embarrassed. "In the city they put our mail through a slot in the door."

"I'm Dr. Cross, by the way, and this is my daughter, Kyla," said the man. "I'm glad to see there are some other children in the neighborhood."

"Your new house is really nice," Sarah said. "Have you seen the creek behind it yet?"

Kyla nodded. "I discovered it yesterday. I was trying to skip stones, but they just plopped down."

"I hope you didn't scare all the fish away," Ernie said rudely. "We want to go fishing."

At that moment a woman came out on the porch and called. "Sounds like your mother needs some help unpacking," Dr. Cross said. He and Kyla hurried back to the house, waving good-bye.

"Do you think we should ask Kyla to join our club?" asked Sarah, who was always quick to make friends.

"No," Ernie said. "She's probably stuck-up because she's rich. And we don't need any strangers poking around."

"She didn't seem stuck-up." Sarah looked again at the imposing house and manicured lawn. Maybe Ernie was afraid Kyla would think his house was shabby by comparison. Sarah shrugged. "But you might be right."

"Come on. Let's get the tent set up," Ernie said.

They walked around the bend in the road to Ernie's house. Ernie went inside to give his mother the receipt. Then they loaded up supplies and headed through the woods to the clearing.

"Mom said the weatherman predicted rain this afternoon," Ernie said. "I hope he's wrong."

Sarah and Marvin looked at the sky. It was perfectly blue, with only a few fluffy white clouds.

"It doesn't look like rain to me," Marvin said. He polished his glasses on the bottom of his shirt. "This is a great spot for a clubhouse." Even though they were just a short way from Ernie's house, the woods encircled the clearing, making it look completely wild.

"This *is* a great spot," Sarah exclaimed.

Ernie unrolled the tent. "Oh, rats!" he said. "I forgot the tent stakes." He dashed back through the woods to his house.

"What's that funny smell?" Sarah asked.

Marvin sniffed the air. "I think it's coming from the creek," he answered. They walked up a slight rise and looked down at the stream.

"Whew." Sarah held her nose. "I don't remember it smelling like this before."

"It's those dead fish," Marvin said, wrinkling his nose and pointing to the fish. "I wonder what could have killed them."

"Do you think the water is poisoned?" Sarah asked.

"What's going on?" Ernie dropped the tent stakes he was carrying and went to stand beside them. "Oh, gross," he said. "Someone must have dumped something in the water."

"Jeepers! That's awful!" Sarah said. "And besides, it's against the law."

"No fishing today," Ernie said with a sigh. "I guess we can't do anything about it."

"We can if we get proof," Marvin said thoughtfully.

"Like pictures," Sarah said, holding up the camera on the cord around her neck. She quickly snapped several pictures of the dead fish.

Marvin climbed down to the edge of the water. "I'll bet this is what did it," he said. He pointed to a small rocky area. A slimy red substance coated the stones.

Sarah took another picture. Then she climbed quickly up the bank. She walked around the clearing with her nose in the air. Every few feet she stopped and sniffed. "It's not too bad here," she said, finally deciding on a spot at the far end, away from the water.

The tent was large, and Ernie had obviously set it up before. With very little help from Marvin and Sarah, the tent was soon erect and the corners tied to stakes.

"This is great," Marvin said as he stood back and admired their work.

"We used to go camping a lot before my dad left," Ernie said. For a second he looked sad. Then he seemed to shrug it off. "If we had some crates or something like that, we could make furniture."

Marvin glanced at the sky. The sun was almost directly overhead. "We'd better get home," he said. "In my note I said we wouldn't be gone very long."

"This would be a great place to camp out for the night," Sarah said casually, while Ernie walked them back to where the twins had left their bikes. She ignored Marvin's look of alarm.

"That might be fun," Ernie answered.

"Would your mom let you camp out?" Sarah asked.

Ernie nodded. "She wouldn't care. I've done it before. She works tonight, but she's off tomorrow night. We could do it then."

He turned to Marvin. "Are you sure you wouldn't be scared?"

"Of course not." Marvin managed to sound confident.

Sarah gave Marvin a sideways glance. "It's not like we believe in ghosts or anything."

FIVE

A New
FRIEND

By the time the twins reached home, Mrs. Pender, the sitter, was grumpy. The Fremonts hired Mrs. Pender to stay with them whenever there was a school vacation, even though both Sarah and Marvin insisted they were too old for a sitter.

"She just sits all day and watches soap operas on television," Marvin often complained to his parents.

"I feel better knowing someone is here in case of emergencies," Mrs. Fremont would answer each time.

The one thing Mrs. Pender did do was cook. Both twins admitted that Mrs. Pender always fixed them an excellent lunch. Today she had prepared homemade clam chowder and apple cinnamon muffins.

"The muffins are better when they are

fresh from the oven," she complained as she reheated the soup. "I thought you'd be home a long time ago."

"We're sorry. We didn't notice how late it was getting," Marvin said. He stuffed half a muffin in his mouth. "These muffins are still the best."

"We were setting up a clubhouse," Sarah explained.

Mrs. Pender's plump face softened. "I had a clubhouse when I was young." Marvin thought she would tell them about it, but she suddenly glanced at her watch. "I'm missing my favorite program," she fretted.

The twins ate and cleared their dishes off the table. "There's an old crate in the garage," Sarah said. "I could tie it to my bike and we could take it to the club."

"Make sure you're home by dinnertime," Mrs. Pender called from in front of the television.

The twins promised and then headed to the garage. Sarah's bike had a rack over the back tire. Marvin found a piece of rope and tied the empty crate on securely. They put three cans of soda inside the crate and rode back to the woods. After hiding the bikes behind the boulders, they started to untie the crate.

"Here comes Kyla," Sarah said, seeing the girl pedaling down Creek Road.

Kyla slowed to a stop. "Hi," she said cheerfully. "I've been unpacking my clothes for the past two hours. I sneaked off to explore before my parents thought of another job for me to do. I *hate* moving," she said, waving her arms dramatically.

"Do you move very often?" Marvin asked.

Kyla shook her head. "This was the first time. Believe me, it was enough. But my dad's happy. He's going to be the administrator of Memorial Hospital."

"Do you think you're going to like it here?" Sarah asked.

"I think so," Kyla answered. "I love the house and the woods. I wish the stream wasn't so yucky, though."

"It's not most of the time," Marvin assured her.

"That's right," Sarah said with a chuckle. "But sometimes it's haunted." She told Kyla about Marvin's claim to have sighted a ghost.

Kyla looked around curiously. "Is that what you two are doing—trying to catch the ghost?"

Before Marvin could speak, Sarah rolled

her eyes and said, "No way. We made sort of a clubhouse," she explained. "We were just taking this crate to be a table or chair."

"Can I see?" Kyla said. Leaving her bike parked next to the twins', she helped Marvin and Sarah untie the crate and followed them to the tent. Ernie was not there.

"Ernie must have gone home for lunch," Sarah said.

"This is really nice," Kyla remarked.

Marvin and Sarah perched on a fallen log, and Kyla sat on the crate. "Is Ernie a good friend of yours?" Kyla asked.

"He helped us solve a mystery," Marvin replied. "There was a car thief in Liberty Corners, and we helped catch him and his gang, too."

"Wow, that sounds like fun," Kyla said. "In the city we had crime, too. But the police did all the investigating."

Suddenly there was a crashing sound in the woods, and then Ernie stepped into the clearing. At the sight of Kyla he scowled.

Kyla stood up. "I'd better get home. My parents will be worried about me, since we don't really know the neighborhood yet."

"Thanks for helping with the crate," Sarah said.

"Maybe you could use some boxes from our move," Kyla offered.

"No thanks," Ernie said. "We've got enough stuff of our own."

There was a moment of awkward silence. Then Kyla waved and walked toward her bike.

"You weren't very nice to her," Sarah scolded.

"I told you. This club is just for us. We don't need anyone else," Ernie said.

A few drops of rain splattered around them. "We'd better get home," Sarah said, looking at the sky. "I hope it doesn't rain very much and ruin our camp-out tomorrow."

"I don't think it's supposed to rain then," Ernie said.

"I've got an idea," Marvin said. "Why don't we come in the afternoon. We could walk up the creek and see if we can figure out where that red stuff is coming from."

Ernie's face brightened. "Good idea. Now we have another mystery to solve."

SIX

Some DETECTIVE WORK

"This is going to be fun," Sarah said happily the next afternoon as she and Marvin carried sleeping bags, a flashlight, games, and snacks over to Ernie's house.

Marvin had been careful to refer to the campsite as Ernie's backyard. While that was technically true, he was afraid his parents would be alarmed if they knew how far away from Ernie's house the campsite actually was. After speaking with Ernie's mother, though, Mrs. Fremont had readily given her permission.

Ernie excitedly greeted them as they lugged their supplies to the clearing. "My mom said she heard on the radio that people are complaining about the water. The mayor said someone's going to investigate. We'll have to hurry if we are going to solve the mystery first."

"It doesn't smell that bad now," Marvin said, sniffing the air.

"Maybe the rain washed some of it away," Sarah offered as they stuffed the sleeping bags and supplies into the tent.

"I wonder if that ghost I saw has anything to do with the creek," Marvin whispered thoughtfully to Sarah. "I mean, what if the ghost was upset because the water was polluted?"

Sarah put her hands on her hips. "Face it, Marvin. You didn't really see a ghost. But if we could find out who's polluting the stream, we might solve a *real* mystery."

"Which way should we walk?" Ernie asked, looking down at the bank.

"The water flows downstream," Marvin said. "So it has to be coming from upstream, toward the highway."

"I knew that," Ernie said. A faint red crept up his face. "I was just checking to see if you did."

With Marvin leading the way, they pushed their way through the tangle of bushes along the bank of Liberty Creek. In some places the walking was easy, as the stream meandered through a meadow dotted with spring flowers. In other places it was more difficult to keep the stream in sight. It twisted and turned through rocks and thick underbrush.

Sarah's camera swung from its cord as she bent to examine some rocks. "I don't see that red stuff."

"The rain couldn't have washed away every trace," Marvin said. He checked the bank and rocks carefully, but it was Ernie who discovered a small red streak on a huge boulder buried in the side of the bank.

"At least we know we're still on the right track," Marvin said.

They passed by a wide curve of the stream. A small cement-block storage building stood on the ground above the stream. "We must be behind Kyla's house," Sarah said.

"Well, hurry up before she sees us," Ernie growled, picking up his pace. "We don't want her snooping around."

"I wish you'd stop being so mean about Kyla," Sarah said. "It wouldn't hurt to be friends with her."

Ernie didn't answer. They cut through the woods to avoid some briers and momentarily lost sight of the water.

After a while, however, the land flattened out again and the woods became thinner.

"We're right beside Mr. Dinkerhoff's factory," Ernie exclaimed.

Sarah stopped to snap several pictures of

dead fish washed up on the bank. They saw another patch of red clinging to the stones along the water's edge.

The factory was closed for the day, although Marvin noticed the back fenders of two cars parked in the shadowy area near the loading dock. The cars were partially hidden by the building, but Marvin could see that one was white and the other black. Mr. Dinkerhoff always drove a beat-up old brown van.

"I hope one of those cars doesn't belong to Alfred," Sarah remarked. "He's really a grouch."

The same thought was running through Marvin's mind. Luckily, Alfred did not appear. The factory looked dingy and run-down. "Mr. Dinkerhoff really should fix up this place," Marvin observed.

"Mr. Snyder's probably right. I don't think he makes very much money," Sarah said loyally.

"Hey, look at this pipe," Ernie suddenly called.

Marvin and Sarah hurried over to Ernie, who was pointing to a pipe coming out of the bank beside the factory. The few drops of water in the pipe appeared clear, but directly above the pipe traces of red were visible on the ground. They stared unhappily at the bank. No one wanted to be the first to admit it, but it appeared the mystery was solved.

"That's strange," Marvin said, peering closer. He took his notebook out of his pocket and scribbled quickly. Replacing it in his pocket, he reached over and wiped his finger along the top of the pipe. A faint smear of red showed on his finger.

SEVEN

An Unwelcome VISITOR

It was a glum trio that returned to Ernie's woods. But they brightened when they trooped into his house and discovered that Mrs. Farrow had ordered a pizza for their dinner.

"Thanks, Mom," Ernie said, looking surprised and pleased at the same time.

"Yes, thank you," said Sarah. "This smells really good."

Mrs. Farrow brushed off their thanks. "I didn't feel much like cooking," she said gruffly, dividing the pizza onto paper plates. After dinner they watched television for a while.

Sarah glanced out the window. "It's going to be dark pretty soon," she announced. "We'd better get back to the camp."

Marvin suddenly looked anxious. "Marvin's thinking about that ghost," Sarah teased.

"Don't you worry, little buddy. I won't let any big bad ghost get you," Ernie said with a grin.

After the children washed up, they told Mrs. Farrow good night. "I'll leave the yard light on and the back door unlocked tonight, just in case you need to come in the house," Mrs. Farrow said.

"We won't need anything," Ernie boasted.

Walking back to the clearing, they discussed the stained pipe.

"I can't believe Mr. Dinkerhoff would do such a thing," Sarah said. "He always seems so nice."

"He is sort of old-fashioned," Marvin said. "But remember when we did that unit on the environment at school? In the old days people didn't think about pollution so much. They just believed nature would take care of everything. Now we know better. These days people worry about garbage and polluted water and the ozone layer. Maybe Mr. Dinkerhoff doesn't realize that whatever he's dumping is doing so much harm."

Sarah looked relieved. "I'll bet if we explain what's happening to the stream, he'll stop doing it."

"I think you're right," Marvin said. "We can talk to him tomorrow."

Now that the problem seemed to be so easily solvable, they turned their attention to an evening of fun. They spent some time by the water, skipping stones and trying, unsuccessfully, to catch a frog. Later the friends planned to play board games by flashlight.

While they sat and talked, Kyla stepped into the clearing. "Hello," she called in a friendly way. "I thought I heard people laughing. What are you all doing?"

"What's she doing snooping around?" Ernie grumbled under his breath.

Marvin couldn't tell if Kyla had heard Ernie.

"I've been thinking. There's a storage building at the back of our property. It would make a great clubhouse," Kyla offered.

"No, thanks," Ernie said sharply. "This is good enough for us. What are you doing here, anyway? This is my woods."

Kyla's smile faded, and she stared at Ernie. "It's my woods, too, you know."

"Maybe you could come to our house sometime," Sarah said.

Kyla nodded. "Well, I'd better go," she muttered after a minute of silence. "See you." She disappeared back through the woods.

"I think we hurt her feelings," Sarah said, staring at Ernie. "You were mean."

"There's not enough room in the tent," Ernie pointed out stubbornly. He looked at the ground. "The three of us get along great," he said unhappily. "Besides, she's a girl."

"I'm a girl," Sarah commented.

"Yeah," Ernie admitted. "But you're interested in catching crooks and stuff that other girls wouldn't like."

"Maybe we should talk to Kyla and find out what she does like," Marvin said.

"Well, it's too late tonight. She's gone." Ernie looked pleased.

It seemed useless to argue. They sat down in a circle. "This is great," Ernie said. His voice echoed loudly in the deepening shadows.

Marvin glanced toward the stream. It was already difficult to see through the dark line of brush under the trees. The wind rustled the leaves, and beyond, the creek bubbled over the rocks. Something, an early rising raccoon, perhaps, scurried under a bush, its eyes a quick flash of light. It was a peaceful scene. Marvin suddenly remembered why he'd been reluctant to camp out. There didn't seem to be anything ghostly hanging about. But now that darkness approached, there was something unsettling in the air. Something that

made the hairs on the back of his neck prickle, so that he shivered slightly.

Ernie glanced around. "It's getting awfully dark."

Sarah looked nervous, too. "Maybe we should get in the tent," she said, rubbing her arms. "I feel a little cold."

Marvin switched on the big flashlight, and the area was bathed in a warm, comforting glow. "I'll bet I can beat you both at Monopoly." He played the light around the woods as he headed for the tent. Then he gasped. Another light weaved through the woods. They could hear the crash of large feet tramping closer and closer. Marvin flashed his light on the trees. Ernie stood up behind him. "Who is it?" Ernie asked in a loud whisper.

The other light had nearly reached the clearing. Marvin took two steps backward and stumbled over a tree root. He fell sprawling on the ground, and the flashlight rolled uselessly away.

For a dreadful moment there was silence, as though whoever, whatever, was waiting to attack. Then, just barely visible in the glow of the fallen light, a large figure loomed out of the woods.

EIGHT

Another VISITOR

Marvin wanted to run. His head sent the message to his legs, but his legs seemed to be made of jelly. The figure was almost upon them. In another second it would be too late.

"Everything okay?" Mr. Fremont stepped out of the woods. "I thought I'd better check on you adventurers." He swung his light around the camp, flashing it over three pale faces. "Uh-oh. Did I scare you?"

"Of course not," Ernie answered weakly. "We were just getting ready to play a game of Monopoly."

Marvin remained sitting on the ground where he had fallen, waiting for his legs to stop shaking. Mr. Fremont leaned down and peeked into the tent. "Hey, this is great," he exclaimed. "Makes me wish I was young again."

He straightened up and looked at his son. "Are you all right, Marvin?"

"Sure, Dad," Marvin said. His legs finally obeyed, and he stood up.

"This is not exactly what I'd call your backyard," Mr. Fremont said to Ernie.

"It's okay," Ernie assured him. "I camp here all the time in the summer."

Mr. Fremont said cheerfully, "Well, okay. I'll see you two in the morning."

Marvin watched his dad's light bobbing away. "I was really scared for a minute," he admitted when his dad was out of hearing distance.

"Me too," Sarah said.

"Not me," Ernie said with a breezy air.

Sarah put her hands on her hips. "You don't fool me, Ernie Farrow. You were just as scared as we were."

Ernie grinned. "Well, maybe a little, just for a second."

It was suddenly very quiet. While they'd talked to the twins' father, darkness had completely surrounded them, like a curtain, shutting off everything except the tiny circle of light from their flashlights.

"Let's go inside," Sarah said, sounding shaky. She crawled through the entrance to the tent and sat on her sleeping bag, setting up the game board.

Inside, the light cast a friendly glow as they played a rather long game of Monopoly and nibbled on several bags of snack food. Sarah ended up with hotels on half of the properties, bankrupting Marvin and Ernie.

"This is fun," said Ernie, stretching out on his sleeping bag.

"We should stay awake all night," Sarah said, and almost immediately fell asleep.

"Hey," Ernie said to Marvin. He sat up and leaned on one elbow. "Is that a comic book in your bag?"

Marvin reached down in his sleeping bag and whipped out two comic books. "You can read this one," he offered generously. "It's my favorite." The cover showed a wolfman with fangs dripping blood.

Ernie took the comic eagerly, but after a few seconds he put it down. "Do you have any funny ones?" he asked, glancing nervously around their shadowy sleeping quarters.

Marvin shook his head. He took off his glasses and placed them carefully in a case. "We'd better go to sleep, too. We want to be sure to wake up early and talk to Mr. Dinker-hoff."

A loud snore was his only answer. Marvin settled into his sleeping bag. Now that it was quiet, the uneasy feeling had returned. He thought briefly about peeking out of the tent, in case the ghost had come back. It was probably too dark to see anything anyway, he told himself. He tossed and turned restlessly, sure he could never sleep. But in spite of the spooky chills down his back, Marvin finally drifted off to sleep.

It was not a peaceful sleep. He dreamed the woods were full of ghosts, wispy creatures with glowing red eyes, drifting from tree to tree. He tried to warn the others, but when he did and they turned to look, the ghosts were gone. Sarah and Ernie were laughing and throwing Monopoly money and hotels in the air. All the time the ghosts were sneaking closer and closer. One of the ghosts suddenly floated in the air over their heads. Then Marvin noticed something even worse. The ghost was wet, and water dripped, dripped down on Marvin. In the dream, Marvin picked up a towel and tried to wipe up all that water. That's when he noticed the water was very red, and very slimy.

NINE

A Watery
GHOST

Marvin sat up, completely awake. They had left the flashlights on, and now one was burned out and the light from the other was very dim. For a second he didn't know where he was. Then he remembered, and at the same time thought of the dream.

He shivered and reached to pull the sleeping bag around him. Marvin froze. It wasn't a dream! The sleeping bag was wet. Frantically he reached for his glasses and put them on.

"Wake up," Marvin yelled at the others. He touched the soggy walls of the tent. "It's raining!"

Sarah was already awake. "Oh, jeepers. The tent is leaking," she moaned.

Through it all Ernie slept soundly, not even waking when a large drip fell right on his nose. Marvin leaned over and shook him until Ernie sat up with a confused look on his face. "What? Is it morning?"

"We're about to be washed away," Sarah said grimly. "It must have been raining for a long time."

"Rats," Ernie groused, thoroughly awake at last. "We'd better make a run for the house."

They gathered up their soaked sleeping bags. Sarah groped around until she found her camera and slung it around her neck. Ernie picked up the one dim flashlight, even though it was almost out. "Ready?" he asked.

They crawled out into the steady downpour. Miserable, wet, and sleepy, Marvin and Sarah stumbled after Ernie toward his house. Suddenly Ernie jerked to a stop so fast that Marvin and Sarah crashed into him. Ignoring their complaints, Ernie grabbed Marvin's arm.

"Do you see that?" Ernie whispered. Even in the faint light from the flashlight, Marvin could see his friend's face was pale. He noticed Ernie's trembling finger and looked at the stream.

Through the sheet of rain Marvin could make out the figure of a man. He was standing so that his face was hidden as he pointed up the creek in the direction of Kyla's house. A faint glow surrounded him, even though he did not appear to be carrying a light.

"Who is that?" Sarah whispered in Marvin's ear.

Slowly the man turned to face them. Marvin glimpsed his ragged clothes and a pale face nearly hidden by his hat. For an instant their eyes met. Then the sudden flash of Sarah's camera startled Marvin, and he glanced away.

"Got him," Sarah muttered.

When Marvin looked back, the figure was gone, melted into a mist that swirled into the dark edge of the trees. Marvin should have been paralyzed with fear, but instead he felt a wave of sadness wash over him.

"Did you see that?" Sarah gasped.

Then Ernie, who had been frozen in silence, screamed, "It's a ghost!" Without waiting to see if the others were following, he crashed through the woods toward the house. Marvin and Sarah pounded behind, not even slowing as branches slapped and scratched them in their mad dash for Ernie's back door. Reaching it at last, Ernie jerked the door open and they fell in, tripping over one another and landing in a heap on the kitchen floor.

Ernie scrambled up and twisted the door lock just as the kitchen light clicked on. Ernie's mother surveyed the scene in astonishment. She tightened the belt on her bathrobe and said, "What is going on? You woke me up."

"G–g–ghost," Ernie stuttered. Then they were all talking at once, trying to make her understand.

"My goodness, you're all soaking wet!" Mrs. Farrow exclaimed. "The weather forecaster never mentioned rain." She went to the bathroom and returned with three big towels. "Could one of your friends be playing a trick on you?" she asked as she passed out the towels.

"None of our friends knew we were camping out," Sarah said.

Mrs. Farrow peered through the windows and then switched off the yard light. "I don't know what you thought you saw," she said. "But I can't imagine anyone out in the woods on a night like this. I never would have let you camp out if I'd known it was going to rain. That old tent always did leak."

Marvin rubbed his hair, grateful to be inside, where it was warm and light. Suddenly Ernie snapped his fingers. "Kyla knew," he

shouted. "I'll bet it was her. She was getting revenge because we didn't let her stay."

Marvin frowned. "It didn't look anything like Kyla."

Ernie shrugged. "She wore a disguise. It had to be her."

"But whoever it was just turned into smoke," Marvin protested. "Didn't you see?"

Ernie blushed. "I closed my eyes. I didn't want to look at that awful face."

Marvin turned to his sister. "He *did* turn into smoke. You saw, didn't you?"

Sarah shook her head. "I was winding the camera. When I looked again, it was gone." She paused. "Maybe it was nothing. I mean, the rain was coming down pretty hard, and it was really dark. Maybe it was only a tree," she added weakly.

"What imaginations you all have," Mrs. Farrow said, shaking her head.

Marvin glared at his sister. "How can you say it was a *tree*? You know there was something there."

"There was something, all right," Ernie said grimly. "But now that I think about it, that was no ghost. I don't know how she did it, but I'm sure it was Kyla."

Sarah looked skeptical. "Her parents

wouldn't let her come out in the middle of a rainy night just to scare us."

"Maybe she sneaked out," Ernie said stubbornly. "I'll bet she's home right now, laughing like crazy."

"It couldn't be her," Sarah said. "She was just moving in when Marvin saw the ghost the first time."

Ernie turned to Marvin. "Did you say anything about the ghost to Kyla when you were talking to her yesterday?"

"Sarah mentioned it," Marvin admitted. "She was teasing me about it."

"I knew it," Ernie crowed.

"But this ghost looked exactly like the one I saw the first time," Marvin said.

"The first time you imagined a ghost," Ernie insisted. "Then when you told Kyla, she decided to copy it and scare us."

"Maybe you saw the ghost of Liberty Corners." Mrs. Farrow chuckled.

"What ghost of Liberty Corners?" they chorused.

"When I was a kid, there were rumors about a ghost that haunted these woods, but I haven't heard them for years," Mrs. Farrow said. She shook her head. "I shouldn't be filling up your heads with nonsense. You know there's no such thing as ghosts."

Sarah patted her camera. "We'll find out tomorrow. If it was a ghost, I think I got a good picture of it."

An hour later they had taken quick hot showers and dried their hair, and they were now tucked in bed. Marvin bunked with Ernie in his room, and Sarah, wearing one of Mrs. Farrow's nightgowns, snuggled on the couch. Mrs. Farrow had made a brief call to Marvin and Sarah's parents, assuring them the children were warm and safe, and the house was at last quiet.

Marvin lay awake, listening to Ernie's snores and thinking. Convinced that it was Kyla playing tricks, and happily plotting his revenge, Ernie had drifted off to an easy sleep. But Marvin knew he was wrong. Even though it had been for only an instant, he had seen the ghost's face quite clearly. What was the ghost trying to tell them? Was he unhappy about the polluted stream? He *was* pointing up the creek. Marvin frowned, trying to remember how the ghost had stood. Kyla's house was around a curve, and it seemed to him the ghost had been pointing more in that direction than toward the Dinkerhoff factory. If that was true, then why? For that matter, why would a ghost care about pollution? Maybe the ghost and the problem in the creek weren't connected at all. It was very puzzling. Marvin was still trying to figure it out when he fell asleep.

TEN

KYLA

Ernie was already up when Marvin awoke the next morning. "We have to figure out some way to get even with Kyla for that ghost trick," he said as soon as he saw Marvin's eyes were open.

"It wasn't Kyla," Marvin said patiently. "And anyway, why would Kyla point toward her own house?"

"To throw us off the track," Ernie said. "Who else could it have been?"

"I think we saw a real ghost," Marvin said. "And I think he was trying to tell us something. After we talk to Mr. Dinkerhoff, let's investigate the ghost."

"Well, I guess we could look around," Ernie said grudgingly. "But it won't do any good."

Fortunately Mrs. Farrow had thrown their

wet clothes in the dryer before going to bed. The boys dressed quickly and headed to the kitchen for breakfast.

The fickle spring weather had changed again. Bright sun streamed through the window curtains, making a polka-dot pattern on the breakfast table. Sarah was seated there, drinking a glass of orange juice. Mrs. Farrow put two boxes of cereal on the table. "You'll have to make your own breakfast," she said. "I have a dentist appointment this morning." She fished her car keys out of her purse and added, "It's too bad your camp-out ended in such a disaster."

Marvin shrugged. "It was fun anyway."

"Do you know anyone who could tell us more about the ghost?" Sarah asked.

Mrs. Farrow shook her head disapprovingly. "I wish I hadn't mentioned it. You could try the library, I suppose," she said. "Mrs. Muncie, the librarian, is really interested in the town's history. I'm sure she could help you."

"That's a good idea," Marvin said, pouring himself a bowl of cereal.

"After breakfast I want you to clean up your camp," Mrs. Farrow told Ernie.

Ernie frowned, but a stern look from his mother kept him quiet.

After breakfast Marvin and Sarah called their parents. "We're going to help Ernie clean up the mess," Marvin told his father. "Tell Mrs. Pender we'll be home by noon."

Then they followed Ernie back to the campsite. To their dismay, they discovered that in their haste to get out they had knocked down the tent. On top of that, they had forgotten to pick up the Monopoly game, and it was ruined.

"Jeepers, what a mess," Sarah said.

Marvin put his finger to his lips, signaling them to be silent. At the same time, he ducked behind the partly collapsed tent and peeked around.

Following Marvin's example, Sarah and Ernie hid, too. Marvin pointed to the creek. A woman climbed up on the bank, carrying two small bottles of water. A man filmed her actions with a large video camera propped on his shoulder.

"That's Nancy Jenkins, the reporter on Channel 5 news," Sarah whispered. "I've seen her on television."

"What's she doing?" Ernie asked quietly.

Nancy Jenkins was obviously not happy. She scraped her shoes on some grass, trying to clean off the mud. She shook her head. "I think the rain has cleaned up the stream."

"We could still show this on the news," the man remarked. "It would let people know that you care about the environment."

Nancy Jenkins nodded. "Let's go back to the station."

They trooped off toward the highway, hardly glancing at the ruined campsite.

"That's too bad," said a voice. They turned to see that Kyla had come into the clearing. "I was worried about you when I woke up this morning and saw that it had rained."

"I'll bet you were worried. Are you sure you weren't out in the rain yourself?" Ernie asked suspiciously.

Kyla folded her arms and glared at Ernie. "What's that supposed to mean?" she demanded.

"We believe we saw a ghost last night," Sarah explained. "But Ernie feels maybe someone was trying to scare us."

"And you think it was me, right?" Kyla asked Ernie.

"You were the only one, except for our parents, who knew we were camping," Ernie said with a scowl.

"It wasn't me," Kyla said. She looked at the others. "Honest. Do you think I'd be dumb enough to run around in the middle of the night scaring people I want to be friends with?"

"I believe you," Sarah said. "Marvin thinks it was a real ghost."

"There is a legend about a ghost in Liberty Corners," Marvin told her. "We're going to the library to see what we can find out."

Kyla's eyes sparkled with interest. "What do you think he wanted?" she asked. Without waiting for an answer, she added, "If there's a ghost around my house, I'd like to know about it. Do you mind if I come with you?"

"You're not afraid of ghosts?" Ernie asked.

"I don't know," Kyla answered truthfully. "I've never met one."

Ernie picked up a stack of soggy Monopoly money. "My favorite game," he said with a sigh.

"I've got an extra one you could have," Kyla offered with a friendly smile. "Last Christmas both of my grandmothers gave me Monopoly." Without being asked, Kyla helped gather soggy bags of snacks and fix the tent.

When they had finished cleaning up, Marvin insisted they return to the creek. He stared at the bank and sighed. "Nancy Jenkins and her cameraman walked all around here. I wanted to check if the ghost left any footprints," he explained. "But there's no way to tell now."

Ernie bent down and examined the prints. "Here's Nancy Jenkins's print. I noticed that she wore shoes with a short, square heel when she wiped them off." He pointed to another print. "This must be the cameraman's. See, his boots had those funny ridges." He looked at Kyla's fresh tracks in the muddy earth. "I don't see any of your footprints near where we saw the ghost," he admitted.

Ernie stood up and looked at Kyla. "I guess I was wrong about you being here last night."

Kyla smiled. "That's okay. I guess I might have thought the same thing if I were you." She laughed suddenly. "Actually, it would have been a pretty funny trick."

Ernie grinned back. "You should have seen us running for the house."

Marvin had been examining the mass of footprints while they talked. Now he stood up. "There are only two sets of prints here. Kyla wasn't here, *and neither was anyone else.* It had to be a ghost that we saw. And I have a feeling he's trying to tell us something about this creek!"

"We better go talk to Mr. Dinkerhoff," Sarah said. She quickly told Kyla about their discovery.

"I guess I'll see you guys later," Kyla said. She started walking back toward the woods. Sarah and Marvin gave Ernie a questioning look.

"Come on with us," he yelled after her gruffly. "I guess four kids ought to be able to outsmart one ghost."

ELEVEN

An Explanation
AND A
PROMISE

At that time in the morning, the parking lot of Mr. Dinkerhoff's factory was full of cars, and several men were busily loading a truck with boxes ready for shipment. One of them was Alfred. He took off the baseball cap he was wearing and scratched the nearly bald top of his head. As he replaced the cap on his head, he spotted the twins, Kyla, and Ernie. He stared as they crossed the parking lot, but he did not try to stop them.

"What are we going to do?" Sarah asked as they approached the door. "Should we knock or just go in?"

Marvin had been wondering about this, too, but fortunately at that moment Mr. Dinkerhoff appeared and spoke to one of the men loading the truck. Seeing the children, he walked over to them.

"This is our friend Kyla," Marvin said politely.

"Any friend of these two is a friend of mine," said Mr. Dinkerhoff, shaking her hand.

"Could we talk to you for a minute?" Marvin asked.

"Such serious faces." Mr. Dinkerhoff chuckled. "What could be so important on a beautiful day like this?"

Mr. Klinger came out of the building and stood beside the older man. "Hi," he said in a friendly voice. As he looked at their faces, his smile faded. "What's the matter?"

"We think that your factory is polluting Liberty Creek," Marvin blurted out.

Mr. Dinkerhoff pulled at his long mustache thoughtfully. "That does sound serious. Why don't you all step into my office and explain." He led the way down a dark, dirty hallway. They passed a large room filled with workers and machinery. Marvin would have liked to stay and watch, but Mr. Dinkerhoff opened a door leading to a small office.

The only furniture in the room was a battered old desk stacked high with papers, a sagging file cabinet, and a number of folding chairs. One wall of the room had several shelves, each full of plastic figures and toys in bright colors. They gave the dingy room a jaunty look in spite of the clutter.

Mr. Dinkerhoff removed some piles of paper from the chairs so they could sit down. Mr. Klinger leaned against the door.

"Now," said Mr. Dinkerhoff. "Begin."

Taking turns, Sarah, Ernie, and Marvin told about discovering the pollution and tracing it back to the factory.

"How did you happen to be near the creek in the first place?" Mr. Klinger interrupted.

"We were going to set up our detective agency there," Ernie answered. "But between the pollution and the ghost, it's been a pretty scary place."

Mr. Klinger seemed startled. "A ghost?"

"Never mind about the ghost, Roger," said Mr. Dinkerhoff sharply. "There have been rumors about a ghost haunting Liberty Corners for generations. It's the pollution that bothers me. If these children say they found pollution coming from our factory, I believe them. How could this have happened? Such a thing might put me out of business. I could be given a terrible fine."

"It was coming out of that pipe near the creek," Ernie said.

A stricken look passed over Mr. Dinkerhoff's face. "Wait. I know how it happened. It was my fault. I forgot to turn off the switch to the dye vat the other night. My nephew told me about it the next morning. If he had not stayed late that night and discovered it, things might have been much worse. Some of the dye must have gone out the overflow drain."

"I knew it had to be some kind of accident," Marvin said. "Nancy Jenkins from the television station was at the creek this morning getting water samples. I think the rain had washed most of the dye away, though."

Mr. Klinger frowned.

"Don't worry," Marvin said. "We won't tell anyone."

"Thank you, children." Mr. Dinkerhoff sounded relieved. "You have my word it will not happen again."

"I'll show them out," said Mr. Klinger. Silently the children trooped after him, leaving Mr. Dinkerhoff in his office.

Mr. Klinger did not speak as he walked down the hallway. "Some people get very forgetful when they're old," he said as they went out the door. "I'm afraid running a factory has become too much for my uncle." Mr. Klinger waved his arms back to the old building. "Look at this place. But when I offer suggestions, he won't listen. I've tried to talk him into staying home and taking it easy. I'm afraid his forgetfulness will cause a serious accident someday. This time he was lucky."

"We didn't know," Sarah said. "He always seems so nice."

"Mr. Dinkerhoff *is* nice," Marvin said. "Is that the dye?" He pointed to several barrels stacked in a corner of a storage area near the door.

Mr. Klinger nodded. "We don't have enough room to keep the unopened barrels inside. We bring one in when we need more dye and attach it to a valve that controls the flow."

Mr. Klinger shook his head. "This factory is not a very safe place for you to be around. But don't worry. I'll try to watch my uncle so nothing happens again."

TWELVE

Checking
OUT A
GHOST

"Jeepers. That's too bad about Mr. Dinkerhoff," Sarah said as they walked away from the factory.

Marvin frowned. "Mr. Dinkerhoff said that he had left the switch on, so it was *his* fault the dye went out an overflow pipe. But that doesn't explain the dye I saw on top of the pipe and on the dirt above it. It seemed as if the dye was poured over the bank."

"Maybe it just splashed," Kyla said.

Marvin shrugged. "Splashed *up*? Maybe you're right. But something else is strange. One of those barrels sitting outside looked as if it had been opened. I could see traces of dye around the side of the spigot on the side."

Sarah shook her head. "It doesn't matter. It's not going to happen again."

"I wonder if that will make the ghost happy," Ernie said.

"That reminds me—I haven't developed the pictures I took last night," Sarah said. "We need to get home and check in with Mrs. Pender."

"I have to go home, too," Kyla said. "Mom and I are going to talk to a new piano teacher this afternoon."

"And Mom wants me home to clean the garage today," Ernie said glumly.

"We'll develop the film. Tomorrow I want to visit the library and see if we can find out anything about the ghost," Marvin said.

After agreeing to meet their friends in the morning, Marvin and Sarah hurried home.

Mr. and Mrs. Fremont had left the house hours earlier. Mrs. Fremont had a job in an insurance office, and Mr. Fremont worked for a large bank downtown. Mrs. Pender was, as usual, parked in front of the television.

Marvin was almost happy to see her, however. His stomach was growling with hunger after their busy morning, and soon the whole house smelled of hamburgers cooking.

"I was getting worried about you two," Mrs. Pender said cheerfully. "Now go wash your hands and come eat."

The meal was delicious, but Marvin and Sarah gulped it down, anxious to develop the picture. After lunch Sarah disappeared into the basement, where she and their father had a small darkroom. Marvin was stuck helping with the dishes. In only a few minutes Sarah was back upstairs.

"That film is ruined," she said in a disgusted voice. "It must have been the rain. None of the pictures came out at all."

"Maybe the ghost ruined it," Marvin said. "In a book I read once, every time someone tried to take a picture of a ghost, the picture didn't develop properly."

"One of your comic books, I suppose." Sarah shook her head. "I think it was just old film."

When Mr. and Mrs. Fremont returned home that evening, the twins recounted their adventures in the storm. They did not mention the ghost or the visit to Mr. Dinkerhoff's factory.

"I'm not sure you should be playing by the creek," Mrs. Fremont said. "I heard on the news that something killed a lot of fish there."

"I think whatever it was has disappeared by now," Marvin answered. "Nancy Jenkins from Channel Five news was taking water samples. She spoke as if the pollution was gone."

"Well, until they discover what it was,

you had better not wade in the creek," Mr. Fremont said.

Sarah exchanged a look with Marvin, but their parents were already talking about something else, and nothing more was mentioned about the stream all evening.

The next morning the sun was shining. As soon as their parents left for work, Sarah and Marvin informed Mrs. Pender they were going to the library. "Be home for lunch," Mrs. Pender reminded them.

They rode their bikes and chained them to the rack outside the library door. Just then Ernie and Kyla arrived, riding together.

The library in Liberty Corners was in an old Victorian house near the town square. It was a large, friendly place, each room filled with books and comfortable chairs. The polished wood floors creaked with age as the children walked to the main desk. The school librarian insisted on complete silence, but that was not the rule here. Two older men sat in one corner chatting over newspapers, and several teenagers were busily working on a project at a large table covered with papers and books. Marvin took a deep breath. "I love how it smells in here."

Kyla sniffed appreciatively. "It smells like books and lemon polish."

"Hello, Mrs. Howard. Is Mrs. Muncie here?" Marvin asked at the desk.

"Hi, Marvin. She's working in the stacks, I believe," the head librarian said with a smile. "Who are your friends? I haven't seen them around before."

"This is Kyla Cross," Sarah said. "She just moved to Liberty Corners."

"Welcome," said Mrs. Howard. "We'll have to get you a library card." She turned to Ernie. "Are you new in town, too?"

Ernie shook his head. "My mom comes here. But I don't read very much."

"I think I can find some books you'd like," Mrs. Howard said. She squinted at Ernie a minute as though sizing him up. "Do you like sports?" she asked. "We've got a great section of books about football, soccer, karate...." She gave Sarah a wink.

"I've just joined the karate club," Ernie admitted, "but what I really like is doing experiments with my chemistry set. Do you have any books about that?"

"I certainly do," said Mrs. Howard. "We'll get you a library card as well."

"Mrs. Howard was nice. I suppose Mrs. Muncie is old and crabby," Ernie said as they walked downstairs to the room where the oldest magazines and books were stored.

Marvin grinned but didn't answer. He watched Ernie's face as they rounded one row of shelves piled high with dusty books and papers and found Mrs. Muncie standing on a ladder, putting some magazines on a shelf.

"Hi, Mrs. Muncie," Marvin called up to her.

Mrs. Muncie jumped. "Oh, you startled me." She chuckled as she climbed down, brushing a cobweb away from her long blond hair. Ernie's mouth fell open. Mrs. Muncie was as pretty as any actress on television.

"Ernie's mom said you know a lot about the history of Liberty Corners," Marvin began.

"My favorite subject," Mrs. Muncie said encouragingly. "What can I help you with?"

"Actually, we wanted to ask you about the ghost of Liberty Corners," Ernie explained.

"Why is everybody interested in that old legend all of a sudden?" Mrs. Muncie said as she pushed the ladder into a corner. "Someone else asked me about that just last night."

"Who was it?" Marvin inquired.

"Oh, just some man," Mrs. Muncie answered. "I didn't know him. He must not use the library very much. He said he was collecting old ghost stories for a magazine article."

Marvin scribbled the information in his notebook. "What can you tell us about the ghost?" he asked.

Mrs. Muncie led the way to her office. She poured herself some coffee from a pot on a warmer on a shelf. Then she pushed aside a stack of old magazines and set her cup down on the desk.

The librarian shook her head. "Not very much at all. People have reported seeing a ghost along the stream since pioneer times. Sometimes he's described as gesturing with a mournful look. But no one knows who he is, although some people think it might be an old man named Henry Jones."

"Who was Henry Jones?" Ernie asked.

"Henry and his brother had a small farm near Liberty Creek way back in the early 1800s," Mrs. Muncie explained. "They didn't get along, and often argued. One day Henry's brother disappeared. Henry said his brother had just picked up and gone, but no one believed him. There had been a terrible storm that day, and no one thought the brother would have left in the middle of it. Also, he hadn't taken any of his things. Henry was accused of killing his brother. He was never tried for the crime because no one could prove it.

They never found the body. After that, no one in the town would have anything to do with Henry, and he became a recluse."

"You mean the ghost was really a murderer?" Kyla asked.

Mrs. Muncie hesitated. "The story about the brothers is true, as far as we know. Of course, the ghost part is only a legend."

Kyla gave her a shrewd look. "Do *you* believe in ghosts?"

Mrs. Muncie blushed. She seemed to be thinking about her answer as she busily stacked up some papers.

"I'm sure it was nothing," she said slowly. "But when I was about your age, I thought I saw the ghost of Henry Jones."

Marvin dropped his pencil. He scooped it up and scribbled furiously in his notebook. "What did the ghost look like?"

"Like an old bum," Mrs. Muncie said briskly. "Which I'm sure is exactly what he was. Then he just vanished. I suppose he ran away when he saw me."

"Where did Henry live?" Sarah asked.

"His farm wasn't too far from where the Dinkerhoff factory is now. On the other side of the creek, though. You can still see the foundation of the cabin. Henry Jones was buried nearby. There's a grave for his brother there, too. It's empty, naturally."

Marvin snapped his notebook shut and tucked it in his pocket. "Thanks for talking to us," he said as the children stood to leave.

"That's quite all right," Mrs. Muncie answered cheerfully. "I always enjoy spending time with my favorite detectives."

Marvin paused thoughtfully at the doorway. "One more question," he said. "Was the man who asked about the ghost an older man, kind of chubby, with a great big mustache?"

"That sounds like Mr. Dinkerhoff," Mrs. Muncie said.

When Marvin admitted that he had been describing Mr. Dinkerhoff, Mrs. Muncie shook her head. "No. Mr. Dinkerhoff is one of our favorite patrons. I know him very well. He comes in every week and checks out an armload of mysteries. It wasn't Mr. Dinkerhoff. This was a younger man. He was tall, thin, slightly bald. I had never seen him before."

THIRTEEN

A Broken PROMISE

Mrs. Pender was stirring a pot of chili on the stove. "You are right on time," she called, setting bowls and crackers on the table. Marvin sat down and took his notebook out of his pocket. All through lunch he stared at it without speaking.

"I bet that man was lying," Marvin said when Mrs. Pender left the room to check what was happening on her favorite soap opera.

"What man?" Sarah asked.

"The one Mrs. Muncie said was interested in the ghost. He told Mrs. Muncie he was a writer. But don't most writers do research? And a writer would surely like to read. So why wouldn't the librarians know him?"

"Maybe he's new in town."

"Maybe," Marvin said. "But how would he

know about the ghost? Mrs. Farrow said she hasn't heard the rumors in years."

After lunch the twins went to Ernie's house. He was waiting on his front porch. A few minutes later Kyla arrived, panting from running.

"Boy, it takes you a long time to eat lunch," Ernie grumbled.

"I had to practice the piano," Kyla told him. "I had a lesson from my new teacher yesterday. She's going to give me singing lessons, too."

"Let's go to the clubhouse for a while," Ernie suggested.

"Do you want to be a singer when you grow up?" Sarah asked while they walked through the woods.

"My aunt is an opera singer. I think my mom and dad want me to be one, too," Kyla replied. "I'd rather be a country singer," she confessed. "But don't tell my parents that. My mom would have a stroke."

Sarah broke into song, copying a current hit. Soon Kyla joined in. The boys covered their ears teasingly. The girls sang even louder.

When they reached the clearing, Ernie climbed on the bank and looked down into the water. Then he groaned. "Oh no. Not again."

Marvin stood beside him. A look of dismay passed over his face. "I can't believe it. Mr. Dinkerhoff promised it wouldn't happen again."

Red scum floated down the stream and coated the rocks along the water's edge. The stench of dead fish made the children hold their stomachs uneasily.

"Should we talk to him again?" Kyla asked.

"It didn't do much good the first time," Marvin said unhappily.

"Let's not tell anyone about this," Sarah said. "At least until we give him a chance to explain."

"Let's go tomorrow," Ernie said. "We've detected enough for one day."

The afternoon was ruined. After promising to meet Kyla and Ernie in the morning, the twins trudged home in silence. They had agreed not to tell anyone, but early that evening they learned some unpleasant news.

"The pollution of Liberty Creek has been traced to Mr. Dinkerhoff's factory," Mr. Fremont said, looking up from the evening newspaper.

"How did they find out?" Marvin asked, with a sinking feeling.

"Nancy Jenkins had those samples analyzed. It was the same kind of dye used at the factory," answered Mr. Fremont.

"The city should close that place down," said Mrs. Fremont, who was slicing potatoes for frying. "It looks so run-down and ugly. And now this. Mr. Snyder is starting a petition requesting the city to condemn it."

"What will happen to Mr. Dinkerhoff because of the pollution?" Marvin asked.

"I'm sure he'll be fined," replied Mr. Fremont. "And I imagine a lot more people will sign Mr. Snyder's petition."

"Does the paper say how it happened?" Sarah asked.

"Mr. Dinkerhoff can't explain it," said Mr. Fremont, scanning the article. "His nephew claims someone accidentally washed the dye down the overflow drain."

"I still don't think Mr. Dinkerhoff did it," Marvin told Sarah later when they were alone.

"He didn't do it on purpose. But you know what Mr. Klinger said about his being so forgetful," Sarah reminded him. "Besides, he admitted that it happened once before."

"Remember when we were talking to Mr. Dinkerhoff the other day?" Marvin said. "He remembered every play of your softball game. And that was back last summer. Also, Mr. Dinkerhoff loves his old factory. I just can't believe he would be so careless—not after being warned."

"We saw it ourselves, though. The pollution started at Mr. Dinkerhoff's factory," Sarah began. Suddenly her hand flew over her mouth. "Oh no," she moaned. "I hope he doesn't think we told on him."

FOURTEEN

Another **GHOSTLY** **SIGHTING**

After dinner Kyla called Marvin and Sarah. "My parents said we could use the shed at the back of my yard for our clubhouse! Do you want to come and look at it? Ernie is coming, too."

After promising their mother they'd be back before dark, the twins raced out the door, Mr. Dinkerhoff's troubles forgotten for the moment. They cut across Kyla's yard, meeting Ernie on the way. Their new friend was waiting at the door of the shed, and they all eagerly followed her inside.

Although Kyla called it a shed, it was a sturdy cement-block building close to the creek. Inside, they found a large, dry room. It was empty except for some wooden boxes. "I think the last owners of the house used this to store gardening tools," Kyla explained.

Sarah's eyes sparkled with excitement. "We could fix this up really neat. We could sweep it all out and wash the windows."

"And we could cover these old crates and make them into furniture," Kyla said. "I'll bet Mom has some old curtains we could hang."

Ernie frowned. "I thought we were going to make a clubhouse, not a dollhouse," he said scornfully.

Sarah defended Kyla. "A clubhouse can look nice."

"I won't put up ruffly curtains," Kyla promised. "I just think it would be better with something on the windows and maybe a rug for the floor."

"I suppose that would be okay," Ernie agreed gruffly.

"It will be getting dark soon," Marvin said, looking at his watch. "We'd better get started."

Kyla had brought cleaning supplies and a huge sack of old curtains and rugs. They all armed themselves with brooms and rags and went to work. Ernie used his broom to whisk away some webs stretched across the ceiling corners. Three spiders, bewildered at the sudden destruction of their homes, scurried down the wall and disappeared through a crack in the floor.

Kyla wiped the windows with some paper towels and glass cleaner. Now that several layers of dirt were removed, the early evening sun, low on the horizon, cast a golden glow that made the room seem warm and bright.

Marvin was hard at work using another broom to sweep the floor. "This place is looking better already," he announced.

Finally they sat down on the floor to rest. Marvin told Ernie and Kyla what Mr. Fremont had read in the paper.

"I keep thinking about the dye being on the bank above the pipe," Marvin said. "I wish I could take another look."

Sarah peeked into the sack and pulled out a set of curtains. "Why don't you and Ernie go do that," she said. "When you get back, you'll be surprised at how good this place looks."

The boys set off, cutting through the woods along the stream. Marvin sniffed the cool evening air. There was enough of a breeze to keep the air fresh.

It was already dark in the dense patches of woods near the water. A faint white mist rolled over the creek, muffling sound. Their voices bounced back to them in an eerie echo. The boys joked and laughed, both unwilling to admit how nervous they felt. Ernie quickened his step and looked around at every shadow.

Ernie grabbed Marvin's arm abruptly. "Did you hear that?" he whispered.

Marvin felt his heart thump. He *had* heard something—heavy breathing, a groan as though someone or something was carrying something heavy. Then a strange metallic sound and the noise of water splashing.

The boys crouched, hiding, and peered around some thick bushes. "Oh no," Ernie gasped. He pointed to a faint glow coming from the creek. It was the ghost. This time Marvin noticed the eerie glow of his bones, like those of some loosely held together skeleton. Although his face was too far away to be seen clearly, Marvin could see ghastly empty eyes. The ghost was dragging something through the water, but Marvin and Ernie did not wait to discover what it was.

Slowly, silently, the boys slipped back through the woods. As soon as they were out of sight of the ghost, they broke into a run and didn't stop until they reached the clubhouse. They burst through the door and slammed it. The clubhouse seemed sturdy and safe. Kyla had fetched an electric lantern from her house while they were gone. Marvin and Ernie paused to catch their breath, relieved by the lantern's comforting glow.

Suddenly everyone was talking at once. "The ghost is out there," Ernie shouted.

Now that Marvin's heart had stopped pounding, he could think. "It is strange, though. This ghost didn't seem the same."

"What do you mean?" asked Sarah.

"It was more like a skeleton," Ernie gasped. "With wormy eyes and blood oozing out."

"I think you've been reading Marvin's comic books," Sarah said, ignoring Ernie's angry look.

Marvin stared out a window. "It is curious that this ghost was different. Even Mrs. Muncie said the ghost looked like an old man."

"All this talk about ghosts is making me nervous," Kyla said. "I think we'd better go home before it gets any later."

Sarah opened the door and glanced around. "All clear," she said with a smile. Even so, she stuck close to Marvin all the way home.

Mrs. Fremont was looking in the refrigerator when they walked in the back door. "Oh dear," she groaned. "I forgot to stop and buy milk after work. There's not enough left for breakfast."

"I'll run down to McNaulty's and get

some," Mr. Fremont offered. "Want to come along, you two?"

"Not me," Sarah said. "I'm going to take a bath."

"Sure," Marvin said. "I'd like to see if there are any new comic books out."

"Be sure not to buy any about ghosts," Sarah teased.

Marvin ignored her and grabbed his light jacket. A few minutes later they parked in front of McNaulty's grocery store. While his father went for the milk, Marvin scanned quickly through the comic books.

"Ready?" said Mr. Fremont, on his way to the cash register.

"Yes. I don't see any I want," Marvin said.

They went through the checkout lane and back to the car. "I feel like a milk shake," Mr. Fremont said. "How about you?"

"That sounds good," Marvin agreed.

There was a fast-food restaurant about a mile down the highway. Mr. Fremont buzzed down the road toward it, chatting about his day at the bank. Marvin was only half listening as he stared out the window. When they passed Mr. Dinkerhoff's factory, Marvin snapped to attention. Mr. Snyder's fancy sports car was in the factory's parking lot.

Next to it was a white car. There was enough illumination from the parking lot lights to see Mr. Snyder standing beside his car, deep in conversation with Mr. Klinger. He rubbed one hand over his slightly balding head as he talked. Mr. Klinger was nodding.

"I wonder why Mr. Snyder is at the factory," Marvin remarked.

"He's probably complaining about the stream being polluted," Mr. Fremont answered.

"Maybe he wants Mr. Klinger to sign the petition," Marvin joked.

As soon as he got home, Marvin jotted down in his notebook what he had seen. He stared at the words for a long time. Something was nagging at the back of his mind. Something he should remember. He was still uneasy when he went to bed.

The following morning Marvin awoke to gray skies that threatened more rain. Mr. Fremont had already left for work, and Mrs. Fremont was buttoning her raincoat when he stumbled, still yawning, into the kitchen for breakfast.

"I think parents should get a spring vacation, too," his mother grumbled while she searched in the front closet for an umbrella.

Finding one at last, she headed for the back door. "Mrs. Pender will be a bit late," she said. "What do you and Sarah have planned for the day?"

"We'll probably work on the clubhouse," Marvin answered, taking a bowl and his favorite cereal from the cupboard.

"Watch the weather," Mrs. Fremont warned as she hurried out the door. "The weatherman has predicted heavy storms."

Sarah entered the kitchen just as the door closed behind her mother. "What are we going to do today?" she asked. She poured herself a bowl of cereal and sat down beside Marvin.

"I want to find out a little more about the ghost," Marvin said seriously. "Maybe it really *is* the ghost of Henry Jones. Why don't we see if we can find the foundation of Henry's house?"

"That sounds like fun," Sarah said. "I'll call Kyla and Ernie and tell them to meet us at the clubhouse."

Mrs. Pender had still not arrived when they were dressed and ready to go. Marvin hastily scribbled a note and propped it on the table. After locking the door, the twins headed for the new clubhouse.

Kyla and Ernie were already waiting. "I

brought an umbrella," Kyla said, glancing at the sky. Then she sniffed. "It smells bad again."

Marvin had also noticed the odor. With a heavy feeling in the pit of his stomach, he pushed through the weeds and crouched by the creek.

Sarah came to stand beside him. "Jeepers. It looks even worse," she said. "It's like every night there is more stuff dumped in here."

"Everyone knows where it's coming from, too," Marvin said. "Let's try to find Henry's house. Mrs. Muncie said it was on the other side of Liberty Creek. Do you think *that's* what the ghost was pointing to? When we saw him the first time, I thought he was pointing toward Mr. Dinkerhoff's factory. But see how the stream curves a little right here?" Marvin stood near the trees and stretched his arm out straight.

In the daylight Ernie was much bolder. "I see what you mean, little buddy," he said. "The ghost might have been pointing across the stream. Let's go check it out."

Marvin searched for a place to cross the water. A short distance away he found a good spot. Several large boulders made a rocky bridge. Here the water had formed a small

cove with a high bank. A huge boulder pro-
truded from the bank and hung precariously
over the water.

The stones looked slippery. Marvin stepped
on one and nearly fell into the water.

"Be careful, little buddy. That water's still
pretty cold," Ernie said.

One by one they inched across the stones
and jumped down on the opposite bank. The
bank on that side was high and muddy. They
found a place to pull themselves up by hanging on to bushes growing along the side.

Kyla wiped the mud off her hands on some
grass at the top and looked ruefully at her
dirty jeans. "How are we going to find
Henry's house?" she asked.

"I have an idea," Ernie said. "Let's spread
out at arm's length. That way we can cover
more area. I saw it in a movie once. They
were looking for a dead body."

The mention of a dead body made them all
glance nervously at one another. Marvin
cleared his throat to steady his voice. "Ernie's
got a good idea," he said briskly.

They stood in a straight line, arms ex-
tended, and slowly walked forward. At times
one of them had to push through some heavy
brush. Then the others waited until they were
lined up again.

"Listen," Kyla said suddenly, when they had walked through the woods almost to the road on the other side. "Do you notice anything strange?"

Marvin stopped. "It's too quiet."

Not a sound broke the utter silence of the woods. The trees loomed sullen and dark against the gray skies. A few drops of rain dripped quietly on the ground. "The birds aren't singing," Sarah said. Her voice echoed hollowly against the trees.

"Well, if the birds won't sing, I will," announced Kyla resolutely. She broke into a loud version of "Oh, Susanna" as she moved toward the road.

After a few steps the others joined her, and the forest seemed to lose its sinister air. By now, however, the rain was becoming quite steady, blowing against them and making it hard to see. Kyla unfurled her umbrella, and the others huddled underneath with her.

They emerged from the woods and crossed a small grassy area. When they reached the road, they stopped and looked at one another in frustration. "We're clear over on Edgewood Road. The woods are spooky, but that's it," Ernie declared.

Marvin looked discouraged. "Let's move over a few feet and walk the same way going back. Maybe we just missed something," Sarah said.

Still singing, they headed into the forest again. Kyla's voice rang clear and sweet, encouraging them on, and they cheerfully passed the umbrella down the line. After a while Marvin stopped. "Look at that," he said, pointing to the remains of a stone chimney nearly covered with vines.

"We found it!" Ernie exclaimed. "I never knew this was here." Forgetting the drenching rain, they explored the area. Standing at a certain angle, they could see the shape of the foundation of a small cabin, although the chimney was the best evidence of its existence.

Suddenly Ernie sprawled flat on the ground. "Ouch," he yelled, grabbing his foot.

Marvin hurried to his friend. Seeing that Ernie was all right except for a skinned spot on his ankle, Marvin leaned down and examined the object Ernie had stumbled over. "That's a tombstone. Mrs. Muncie was right. This must be Henry's grave."

FIFTEEN

Flash
FLOOD

The stone was tipped and hidden under a mat of weeds and vines. Working together, the friends managed to clear away enough brush to see the faint letters nearly worn away by time and weather.

"This has to be Henry's grave," Sarah said. "Look, you can make out an *H*, and here's an *R* and a *J* for Jones, and a date—1839. Jeepers, that's over a hundred and fifty years ago."

Marvin was still clearing brush from the site. "Here's another stone," he yelled. He squinted at the lettering. "I think it says *Charlotte Jones, 1848.*"

"I found another one," Kyla said. "I can't figure out the date, but you can still see part of the name."

"It's a family graveyard," Sarah said. "But

everyone must have forgotten about it. No one's tended it for years." She took her camera from her pocket and snapped several pictures of the graveyard.

Silently they stood for a moment, staring at Henry's grave. "This place gives me the creeps," Ernie finally said.

Disappointed, Marvin said, "I guess I thought we'd find some kind of big clue here."

"Well," said Kyla, "we've learned the identity of the ghost. That's pretty big."

"I know," Marvin answered slowly.

"Maybe Henry wanted someone to clean this graveyard up. When the weather's nicer, we should bring some flowers and pull these weeds," Kyla suggested.

"We'd better get back home," Marvin said, shivering in the wet, cold weather.

The rain began to fall much harder, coming down in thick sheets too fast for the ground to absorb. Kyla's umbrella was almost useless, and the wind whipped the rain until it was nearly impossible to see. "It's really getting bad," Ernie shouted over the noise of the storm.

"We've got to cross the creek to get home," Marvin yelled as he sloshed past a deep puddle. He pushed his way through the brush and stared down at the stream in dismay.

The normally peaceful creek, now an angry, swirling brown, was already spilling over the bank. The stones they had used to cross only an hour or so before were completely hidden under the water.

"What are we going to do?" Kyla wailed.

Marvin hesitated. The warm, dry safety of the clubhouse was only a few feet away. But they had to cross the creek. "Come on. The longer we wait, the worse it's going to get." He started to climb down the steep bank to the rushing waters below.

Suddenly the wind seemed to shift slightly, and a white fog drifted along the bank. A prickly feeling that had nothing to do with the weather crept up Marvin's back. He looked to see if the others felt it.

They seemed frozen to the spot. "It's the ghost," Kyla gasped.

The rain lashed down, making it impossible to see. Then a loud *crack* sounded behind them from the dark forest. With a terrible groan a large tree fell toward the creek, missing them by inches.

"That ghost is trying to kill us," yelled Ernie.

"No, wait," Marvin said, pointing to the stream. The tree had fallen straight across it, making a bridge several feet above the swirling waters.

From up the stream came a roar, then a wall of water. "Marvin, get up here!" Sarah screamed. The others helped Marvin scramble to the safety of the high bank just as the water roared past, pushing tree branches and other debris ahead. Miraculously, the waters passed under the fallen tree, and it remained firmly in place. In an instant the flood had passed, thundering its way farther downstream, leaving a dangerously deep whirlpool of muddy water.

"If the tree hadn't fallen when it did, we would have been caught in that," Marvin said. The fog seemed to melt back into the shadowy darkness of the trees. "Thank you, Henry," Marvin yelled.

"Do you really think Henry saved us?" Sarah asked doubtfully.

"Didn't you feel it?" Marvin said stubbornly. "He was here."

"We'd better get across that stream and get home before our parents kill us," Ernie said gruffly.

One at a time they crawled across the makeshift wooden bridge. Then, slipping and sliding on the opposite bank, they hurried to the clubhouse.

"We can stay here until the rain dies down a little," Sarah said. "We're already soaked."

After a few minutes Marvin looked out the windows. "It's hardly raining now. Look."

Kyla glanced down at her muddy tennis shoes. "My mom's not going to be happy when she sees these," she said ruefully.

"Maybe we'd better not tell anyone what happened," Ernie said. "Parents have a way of getting excited when their kids are caught in floods."

Kyla giggled. "Do you think they'd believe that we were saved by a ghost?"

Suddenly they were all laughing. "Maybe we'd better not mention that, either," Marvin said.

Taking advantage of the break in the storm, the detectives hurried home. The twins found Mrs. Pender watching television as usual. She looked up and frowned when they trooped into the house, muddy and wet. "Where have you been?" she scolded. "I was almost ready to call your parents."

Luckily she believed their story about being caught in the clubhouse until the worst of the rain had subsided. She made them change into dry clothes and then sat them down to steaming bowls of vegetable soup.

Sarah crumbled bits of crackers in her bowl.

"How can you eat soggy crackers?" Marvin said, tasting his own soup.

Mrs. Pender had gone to the living room to watch more television. "Come quickly," she called, before Sarah could think of a snappy answer. The twins rushed to the living room. A special bulletin was on the television. "Liberty Creek was swept by a flash flood," the announcer said. The screen showed the floodwater racing downstream. "Fortunately no one was hurt," continued the announcer, "although a bridge was damaged outside of town."

"Jeepers, look at those great pictures," Sarah said. "I wish I had taken one of the flood."

"In other news about Liberty Creek," the announcer went on, "because of continuing complaints about illegal dumping by the Dinkerhoff factory, two agents from the Environmental Protection Agency were to have begun an investigation today. But authorities believe the current storm may have washed away any evidence."

"Humph," snorted Mrs. Pender. "I've

known Jonathan Dinkerhoff for forty years. He would never dump anything in the stream."

"His nephew says he's getting very forgetful," Sarah said.

"I don't believe that for a minute," Mrs. Pender said. "I talked to him just the other day. He was perfectly fine."

Another soap opera started, and Mrs. Pender seemed to forget all about them. Marvin looked thoughtful as he went back to the kitchen and studied his damp notebook.

"Mrs. Pender may be right," he said, buttering a piece of bread to eat with his soup. "But if it's not Mr. Dinkerhoff, then who is doing it?"

"It's too bad we can't set some kind of trap and catch the criminal red-handed," said Sarah. She grinned. "Red-handed. Get it?"

"I get it," Marvin said absently. "That just gave me an idea for a trap."

"You heard the news. All the evidence was washed away, so Mr. Dinkerhoff can't be fined for polluting the stream."

"Exactly," Marvin said. "The announcer said that two investigators are here. That means that if someone wants to get Mr. Dinkerhoff in trouble, they've got to do it again, and soon, while the agents are still in town."

"So what's your idea?" Sarah asked.

"I'll tell you later," Marvin said as he carried his dishes to the sink. But their plans were put on hold by Mrs. Pender, who insisted that they stay in for the rest of the afternoon.

A telephone call from Kyla revealed that she was under similar restraints. "My mom was really upset about my wet clothes," she confessed glumly. "She says my tennis shoes are ruined."

Although the rain had stopped, a wild wind, strong enough to roll the empty garbage cans down the driveway, was still blowing. Marvin slipped on his jacket and went outside to rescue them before they got into the street. When he returned to the house, his hair was scrambled from the wind, and he was grinning.

"What are you so happy about?" grumbled Sarah.

"A wind like this should dry everything up pretty fast," Marvin said gleefully. "We need to be able to camp out again to have my plan work."

Eyeing Mrs. Pender, still happily watching her television programs, Sarah motioned

Marvin to follow her to her room, where they could talk without being overheard.

"All right," she said, closing the door. "What's the plan?"

"It was your remark about catching them red-handed that gave me the idea," Marvin said. "The dye barrels are stored by the door on the loading dock. I noticed the other day that one of them had been opened. I could see red dye spilled on the outside. I think someone is deliberately dumping dye into the creek. And I'd like to bet they are taking it from that barrel. What if there was fresh dye on the outside of the barrel?" Marvin proposed. "Someplace you wouldn't see it, like on the spigot handle. In the dark the person probably wouldn't even notice. If someone dumps dye in the stream again and has red hands, that will prove they're guilty."

"You're a genius," Sarah said.

"First thing in the morning we'll go talk to Mr. Dinkerhoff," Marvin said thoughtfully. "We need his help to get the dye on the outside of the barrel."

Sarah paused. "I don't think that Mr. Dinkerhoff is guilty," she said. "But maybe we shouldn't tell him, either. That way we'll know for sure."

Marvin frowned. "You're right. To be fair, we shouldn't tell him. And maybe the red dye isn't such a good idea, either. It needs to be something the polluter couldn't get on his or her hands any other way."

Sarah nodded. "Why don't we call Ernie? Maybe he can make something with that chemistry set besides invisible ink."

SIXTEEN

Some DANGEROUS PLANS

As soon as breakfast was over, everyone met at the clubhouse, and Marvin explained his idea to Kyla and Ernie. Just as Marvin had predicted, the wind had dried up much of the rain. Although it was still muddy in shady places, it was almost as though the storm had never happened.

"Do you think you could mix something up?" Marvin asked Ernie.

"I already *have* mixed something up," Ernie confessed with a rueful smile. "When I was working on my own formula for invisible ink, I mixed a bunch of stuff together. It took me three days to wash it off my hands. It's black. Is that okay?"

"I think so," Marvin said. "It'll only be on the spigot. When we find out who has black hands, we'll have all the proof we need."

Kyla reached into a brown paper bag and brought out four huge oranges from home. "I've been thinking about your plan, Marvin," she said as she passed one to each friend. "The dye on the outside of the barrel is a good idea, but I think we ought to be there. What if whoever it is manages to wash the dye away by morning? Or what if the person just says it got on his or her hands at work?"

She picked off the last piece of peel and started breaking her orange into bite-size pieces. "I think we need to hide out someplace and watch," she said, popping a juicy orange section in her mouth.

Marvin stared at her. "How could we do that?"

"It's still too damp to camp out, so you ask to spend the night at Ernie's house," Kyla explained patiently. "Then I'll ask Sarah to spend the night with me. I think I can talk my parents into letting us sleep in the clubhouse. As soon as Ernie's mom goes to sleep, you sneak out and meet us. Then we'll walk to Mr. Dinkerhoff's factory."

Ernie looked nervous. "I've got some real good walkie-talkies," he offered bravely. "We could keep in contact that way."

"Our parents are going to ground us for fifty years if they find out," Sarah said.

"We've got to go tonight," Marvin said. "Tomorrow is the last day of spring break. Mom and Dad would never let us stay over on a school night." He threw his orange peels in the bag and stood up.

"Ernie, you and Kyla better go check with your parents. If all goes well, we'll meet at midnight."

Marvin and Sarah started back to their own house. Just as they crossed the road, a black sports car passed. Mr. Snyder stopped the car and rolled down his window. "I hope the flood didn't ruin your camp," he said.

"We set it up pretty far from the creek," Sarah said. "I think it's all right."

"Camping out like that sure sounds like fun. Makes me wish I was young again." He rolled up his window partway and then stopped. "Maybe you should stay away from the creek until this pollution problem is cleared up. It can't be too healthy."

"The creek really isn't polluted anymore. All that rain cleared it up," Sarah informed him.

"Well, even so, I think it's a shame. Mr. Dinkerhoff should be more responsible. It's bad enough we have to put up with that ugly factory. Did you know there used to be a hotel there? It was built in 1870," Mr. Snyder continued. "I read about it in a magazine. It was quite elegant. There was a famous rose garden with paths for the guests to stroll."

"That sounds neat," Sarah said. "It's too bad it's gone."

Mr. Snyder nodded. "Liberty Corners is growing. I've heard that one of the better motel chains is interested in locating here. Wouldn't it be nice to have a brand-new motel across the street, where the old hotel used to be? Dinkerhoff's is such an eyesore for the community. I can't help but feel the whole community would be less polluted if it were gone."

Mr. Snyder roared off down the street. Marvin frowned. "I wonder how he knew we were camping out."

"We probably told him that day at the store," Sarah answered.

Marvin shook his head. "I don't remember telling him." Again he had a nagging feeling, as though there was something he should remember.

"You must be getting as forgetful as Mr. Dinkerhoff," Sarah teased.

Marvin stared darkly at Mr. Snyder's car as it turned a corner. "Maybe neither one of us is forgetful," he said.

SEVENTEEN

A Midnight INVESTIGATION

Shortly before midnight Sarah's voice crackled over the walkie-talkie. "I think the coast is clear. Kyla's parents are asleep. The lights went out in her house almost an hour ago. We're going to start walking down the stream toward you."

"All right," Marvin said. "Everything is quiet here, too. We'll watch for you." The boys slipped out of Ernie's back door, careful not to wake his mother. Using a flashlight to find their way in the almost moonless night, they walked to the edge of the creek. It was cool, but they were dressed warmly enough to be comfortable.

Ernie tipped back his head and looked at the sky. "Too bad the clouds are covering the stars. It sure is dark."

Marvin's stomach felt jittery. He also

117

wished there was more light. At last they heard crashing sounds in the woods.

"Are you there?" Sarah asked in a hoarse whisper.

"Here we are," Marvin said, trying not to let anyone hear the relief in his voice.

A light bobbed through the trees, and a minute later the girls were standing beside them. "Let's go," Sarah said, leading the way.

"We'll have to be a little more quiet," Marvin said as he followed her.

"Yeah," Ernie snorted. "I could hear you guys coming a mile away."

"It was scary, walking in the woods like that," Kyla confessed. "We wanted to make sure any ghosts would hear us coming and have time to get out of the way."

"You guys quit talking about ghosts," Ernie growled.

They worked their way through the woods until they reached the field behind Dinkerhoff's factory. The light from the parking lot cast a shadowy glow near the loading dock where the dye was stored. The wind blew a paper across the pavement, and the skittery sound made them all jump. The factory appeared deserted.

"I don't think this was such a good idea,"

Ernie whispered. "What if the polluter doesn't come tonight?"

Marvin strained his eyes, looking for a place to hide. "I think he will. Whoever it is knows those investigators are in town." He pointed to some trees and bushes near the creek. "Let's hide behind those."

Sarah slid a backpack off her shoulders and reached inside for an old blanket. She spread it on the ground for them to sit on. "Good thinking," Marvin said, arranging himself so he could see.

"Did you rub the goo on the spigot?" Kyla asked.

"Yeah," Ernie said. "Marvin and I sneaked up and did it right after dark."

"I hope none of our parents try to check on us at home," Sarah said.

The four detectives fell silent, watching intently for any sign of movement. The minutes dragged by. In spite of the tense situation, Marvin found himself unable to keep his eyes open. He peeked at the others. Ernie was already asleep. Sarah's eyelids were drooping, and Kyla's head kept nodding forward.

Several hours later Marvin awoke. He glanced at the glow-in-the-dark numbers on his watch and groaned. He pulled Sarah's arm gently.

His sister sat up, looking startled. "Is someone here?" she whispered.

"We all fell asleep. It's nearly four in the morning," Marvin said. "I guess I was wrong. No one's going to come. We might as well go home."

Sarah shook the others. Grumbling softly and gathering up their things, they got ready to leave. "I hope the polluter wasn't here and we slept right through it," Kyla said.

"Shh." Marvin held up his hand. "Did you see something?" The four detectives froze, not even daring to breathe. A shadowy figure slid around the corner of the building and inched along toward the loading dock.

"Who is it?" Sarah whispered.

"I think I know," Marvin said, "but I can't see for certain."

"Wait." Kyla grabbed Marvin's arm. "There's someone else."

A second figure walked boldly past the building. For a minute both men were hidden in the darkness of the loading platform. Then they emerged holding a large bucket between them.

One of the men carried a small flashlight,

shining it on the ground as they walked. In the faint light the luminous glow of bones became visible, and an empty-eyed face shone under a black hood.

"It's the ghost," gasped Ernie, poised to run.

Marvin grabbed his arm, holding him quiet. "It's a costume," he whispered. Suddenly he sucked in his breath. "I knew it," he said. As the men walked, the light had swung slightly to one side, allowing Marvin to see the face of the second man. Marvin crouched down further behind the bushes. "It's Mr. Snyder."

EIGHTEEN

A Fake GHOST

The fake ghost was obviously unhappy. "Why don't you go wading through that water? It's not much fun, you know."

"Stop complaining," Mr. Snyder growled. "I'm paying you enough to put up with a little discomfort. This should be the last time. A call in the morning to tip off those environmental investigators, and Dinkerhoff should be out of business."

"I still don't know why I have to wear this stupid outfit," the "ghost" said. "I scared those kids enough last time. They won't be camping out near that stream again."

"I'm not taking any chances. Another look at you should be enough to send them running for good. We wouldn't want anyone figuring out what we're doing, now, would we?"

There was something familiar about the fake ghost's voice. Marvin strained to listen as the two men came closer to the bushes. "My foot's asleep," Ernie whispered. He shifted slightly. "That's better—it's starting to tingle." He crouched back down, but as he did, his hand pressed too hard on a stick. It snapped with a loud crack.

"What was that?" Mr. Snyder said. He grabbed the flashlight from the "ghost" and shined it toward the bushes. "Who's there?"

"Run," shouted Marvin, leaping forward. Kyla and Sarah reacted instantly, jumping up and following Marvin. Ernie, hampered by his still-tingling foot, limped slightly behind.

"Get them," Mr. Snyder yelled. He dropped the bucket, spilling the dye uselessly on the weedy ground. With a bellow of rage, the two men plunged into the woods after the children.

"Don't turn on the flashlights," Sarah warned, panting. In the dark Marvin and his friends tripped over branches and rocks, scratching and bruising themselves. The two men traced their frantic flight easily by the sounds.

"Wait," Marvin gasped, reaching for his sister. "The creek. At least we won't break our legs."

Holding hands to keep from losing each other, they slipped into the icy water and plunged down the stream. Ernie and Kyla waded in, too. Behind them they could hear the two men searching the woods.

"Slow down," Ernie whispered from behind. Marvin, still leading the procession, instantly understood. If they walked slowly, the sounds of their progress would be hidden by the normal gurgling of the stream.

Marvin's feet were freezing inside his sopping sneakers. But for a moment he allowed himself to breathe easier. The trick seemed to have worked. Although the men were close by, they were still searching the woods. Marvin didn't dare climb out of the water for fear of running into the men. Grimly he kept on.

"We should have run toward the shopping center," Kyla whispered. "There might have been someone there to help us."

"Not this late," Marvin said. "We've got a better chance hiding here."

Kyla grabbed Marvin's arm. "Do you remember that big boulder sticking out of the bank where we crossed the stream? This afternoon I went back and noticed that it had fallen down in the creek. And then, right behind it, I saw an opening to a little cave! There must have been mud blocking it before, but the flood washed it out. Maybe we can hide there until they give up."

"Can you find it in the dark?" Sarah whispered.

"All we have to do is keep walking until we come to the boulder," Kyla explained.

"Hurry," Ernie groaned. "My feet are cold."

Suddenly Marvin stopped. He listened intently. "Where are those men? I don't hear them anymore."

The only sound was the wind gently rippling through the trees. Somewhere far off, an owl hooted. "I don't like this," Ernie said.

"Maybe they gave up," Sarah offered hopefully.

"I doubt it," Marvin said. "Mr. Snyder knows we recognized him."

Kyla pushed in front of Marvin. "Come on. It's not much farther. At least we can get out of this freezing water."

They followed the creek around a little bend. The banks were higher here and slippery with mud. At last the dark shape of the fallen tree loomed before them. They ducked under it.

"It should be right here," Kyla whispered, peering ahead intently. "There," she said, pointing triumphantly.

The boulder was huge enough to partly block the creek. Water swirled around it. The moon had slipped from behind the clouds, and there was just enough light to see a small opening along the bank. Kyla crawled in a few inches. "Wait. I'll see if it's big enough for all of us," she said. Shivering, the others waited in silence. A second later she poked her head out of the opening. "I can't tell how far back it goes," she said. Her voice echoed weirdly from inside the cave. "But it's dry and we'll all fit." Following her lead, Marvin, Sarah, and Ernie left the icy water and crowded together.

"This would be neat if we could see," Ernie said. "I've never been in a cave before. Maybe we should turn on a flashlight."

"Not yet," Marvin warned. "If those men are anywhere around, they're sure to see it."

"I hope no animals live in the cave," Sarah said, nervously glancing back into the dark hollow past the opening. She tried to find a more comfortable place to sit. "There must be a bunch of tree roots right here," she said as she felt around the cave floor. Suddenly she let out a funny-sounding squeak. "Kyla, where's your flashlight?"

"It's in my pocket," Kyla answered. "But I don't think we should turn it on yet. Marvin's right. Those two crooks might be nearby."

"I think you had better turn it on for a second, anyway," Sarah said in a strangled voice. "I think there is someone else in this cave."

NINETEEN

A Scary DISCOVERY

Kyla fumbled for her flashlight and flicked it on, twisting her body at the same time so the light couldn't be seen from outside the cave. Then both girls screamed and Ernie jumped up with a loud yelp.

"What is it? I can't see," Marvin said. As Ernie moved, Marvin too saw the frightening object on the cave floor. The flashlight gleamed on white bones jumbled against a boulder. It was a skeleton, a real one this time. Bits of frizzy hair still clung to the crumbling skull.

"I was sitting on it." Sarah shuddered. "I was sitting on a skeleton."

"Do you think Mr. Snyder killed someone?" Ernie gasped.

Marvin stared at the skeleton. Now that the shock of finding it had worn off, he was

more curious than afraid. "Whoever that was, he died a long time ago," he said, examining the pieces of clothing that hung on the skeleton. With an exclamation he scraped the dirt off an object on the cave floor. "It's an old pocket watch."

"Better not touch it," Ernie said. When the others stared at him, he shrugged, looking embarrassed. "Maybe it's cursed or something."

Marvin finished rubbing away the caked mud. "Don't be silly. The skeleton is just someone who died a long time ago. I've got a pretty good idea who it is, too."

Kyla aimed her light at the rusty watch. "T. Jones," Marvin read. "This must be Henry's brother. No wonder they never found the body. It's been in the cave all this time."

"Do you think Henry killed him and hid the body here?" Sarah asked.

"Maybe," Marvin replied. "But I'll bet his brother was drowned. Maybe he got caught in a flash flood, like what happened the other day. Maybe his body got washed into this little cave, and got covered by the rocks and mud that washed in and covered the opening. That's why he was never found."

"Maybe they can do tests and find out," Ernie said. "Poor Henry. Everyone thought he killed his own brother, and it was probably just an accident."

Sarah rocked back on her heels. "Wouldn't it be nice if he could be buried in that old graveyard with the rest of the family? Maybe now he can rest in peace."

"I don't get it," Ernie said. "Was the ghost Henry or his brother?"

Marvin leaned back against the muddy cave wall. He was tired and wet. "I believe it was Henry. He's been waiting for all these years for someone to prove he was innocent."

"How long do you think we should stay here?" Kyla asked, with an unhappy glance at the bones. She sat against the cave wall, as far away from the skeleton as she could get.

"We should stay until morning," Sarah said. "That way we'll be sure Mr. Snyder and his fake ghost friend are gone."

"They've probably given up by now," Ernie said. "I don't want to spend any more time in a cave with a dead person."

Suddenly a shadow loomed across the cave entrance. A flashlight beam illuminated the leering skeleton face peering in at them. "I can help you with that problem," the fake ghost said menacingly. "Maybe you won't have to stay in your cozy little hiding spot after all."

TWENTY

TRAPPED!

The fake ghost crouched in front of the entrance, blocking escape. "It's too bad you kids had to get so snoopy. If you had just minded your own business, this whole thing would have been over soon, and no one would have been hurt."

"Except Mr. Dinkerhoff," Marvin retorted, sounding braver than he felt. As he spoke, his mind searched frantically for a way to escape. Perhaps the four of them could overpower the hoodlum if they all jumped at him at once.

The man seemed to read Marvin's thoughts. He reached into his cloak and pulled out a small revolver. "Don't try anything funny," he said, stepping back a bit.

"W-what are you going to do to us?" Ernie's voice shook.

The man hesitated. "I haven't decided." He

cast a nervous glance over his shoulder. "Why is it so cold all of a sudden?" he demanded.

It *was* colder. Marvin shivered. A wispy fog seemed to creep through the cave, bringing with it a clammy chill. The man outside the cave appeared startled. He swung around, pointing his gun. "W-who's there?" he stammered.

Fog swirled around the man's feet. The air was heavy and silent. "What are you kids trying to pull?" he yelled. Then, realizing that the unearthly atmosphere could not possibly have been caused by the cave's occupants, he panicked.

The fog twisted around the man like a blanket, making him invisible. "What's happening?" Ernie whispered hoarsely. "I can't see."

"I think it's Henry," Sarah gasped. It was so cold now that her breath made tiny puffs when she spoke.

The man was slowly backing away from the cave. His foot slid on the slippery mud and he splashed to his knees in the creek, dropping his gun in the muddy water. "That's it," he shouted. "Snyder can take care of his own problems." Scrambling to his feet, he plunged down the creek, stumbling and falling. Marvin listened until the sounds of his retreat faded in the distance.

"Let's get out of here while we have a chance," he said, grabbing Sarah's hand and pulling her with him through the cave entrance.

"Wait." Kyla spoke for the first time since the fake ghost had appeared. She crawled through the entrance and straightened up, balancing herself on the bank. "He's gone." Rays of sunlight were just peeking over the horizon.

Marvin suddenly realized that he was not as cold. The fog had disappeared, and along with it the unnatural silence.

Using some branches from a low-growing bush for balance, Marvin climbed up the slippery bank and stood. Only a few feet away from him was the ghostly figure they had seen before. Marvin thought a faint smile crossed the ghost's face. Marvin was aware of Sarah behind him, just pulling herself over the bank. "Sarah," he whispered. "It's Henry." But in that instant the ghost vanished, melting into the fog so quickly that afterward Marvin was never sure that he had really been there.

"Where?" Sarah asked, peering into the trees.

Marvin sighed. "I guess I was just imagining things. Let's get out of here before that guy decides to come back."

"Let's go to my house," Ernie was saying to Kyla. "My uncle's a police detective." The two were already heading into the woods. Without a pause Sarah and Marvin followed, walking quickly until Ernie's house came into view. Sunlight was spreading as they reached the door and stumbled in.

Mrs. Farrow was just getting up. She was not pleased to hear of the night's adventures. She immediately called the Liberty Corners police station and asked to speak to Ernie's uncle Ned. "He'll be here in a few minutes," she said as she hung up the phone.

While they waited, Mrs. Farrow gave them a good scolding. "No more sleepovers for you, Ernie Farrow," she declared sternly. "I imagine your parents are going to be equally unhappy," she told Marvin, Sarah, and Kyla. "The very idea of you children running around the woods at night! I would have thought one of you might have had more sense."

"We were trying to help Mr. Dinkerhoff," Marvin said weakly.

They were saved from further scolding by the arrival of Uncle Ned. The story was repeated, although the adults looked skeptical when they mentioned Henry's ghost.

"That's very interesting," Uncle Ned said. "I had just arrived at the station when we got the call that Mr. Dinkerhoff had been dumping in the creek again. I was on my way to meet the environmental investigators at the factory."

The four detectives exchanged glances. Mr. Snyder must have gone back to the factory to dump the dye, leaving the "ghost" to track them down.

"But that's a lie," Marvin protested. "It wasn't Mr. Dinkerhoff. Who made the report?"

"Snyder. He says that on Sundays he always goes to his store at the crack of dawn to catch up on paperwork. He claims he actually saw Mr. Dinkerhoff pouring dye into the creek."

"You don't believe him, do you?" Kyla sounded indignant.

"I believe you," Uncle Ned said. "It will be hard to prove, though. Mr. Snyder is a respected member of the community. It will be his word against a bunch of kids who say they saw him in the dark. I wish we had some other kind of proof."

"Maybe we do," Marvin said. He explained quickly.

TWENTY-ONE

A Ghost

CONFESSES

Ernie's mother promised to call the Fremonts and Kyla's parents, and the detectives piled into Uncle Ned's police car. In a matter of minutes they had reached the factory.

"Now, don't say anything until I tell you," Uncle Ned warned as they got out of the car.

The two investigators, looking sleepy and cross, were questioning Mr. Dinkerhoff, who was shaking his head unhappily. Mr. Snyder was close by.

"I tell you that barrel was on the loading dock," Mr. Dinkerhoff was saying. "I don't know how the dye got in the creek."

"I'm shocked that you would do such a thing," Mr. Snyder said. He looked a bit startled to see Marvin and his friends, but he recovered quickly. He leaned against the building and shook his head sadly. "Liberty

Creek is such a pleasant place. I can't imagine anyone wanting to ruin it." Mr. Snyder kept one hand in his jacket pocket as he talked. Marvin glanced knowingly at Detective Farrow.

Ernie's uncle shook his head slightly, warning Marvin to stay silent.

"The creek is a treasure that needs to be protected for the next generation," Uncle Ned said. "Don't you agree, Mr. Snyder?"

"Exactly," Mr. Snyder said. "I know these children like to camp out now and then. That's why I felt I had to report it, even though I hated to make trouble for Mr. Dinkerhoff."

"But I would never do such a thing." Mr. Dinkerhoff was wringing his hands in worry.

Just then a car pulled into the parking lot, and Mr. Klinger jumped out. Marvin noticed a look pass between Mr. Snyder and the new arrival.

"What's the matter, Uncle Jonathan?" Mr. Klinger asked. "Someone called me and said you were accused of polluting the creek again."

Mr. Dinkerhoff was clearly miserable.

"My uncle is quite old," Mr. Klinger said. "I'm sure he would never deliberately do anything to pollute the stream. But sometimes he's a little forgetful." He put his arm around Mr. Dinkerhoff protectively.

Marvin could no longer remain quiet. "We know it was you last night, Mr. Snyder."

Mr. Dinkerhoff appeared startled. The two investigators stopped their questioning and listened.

Mr. Snyder said indignantly, "I have no idea what you're talking about, young man. I was home in bed all night."

"You've been dumping in the creek, trying to put Mr. Dinkerhoff out of business. You had someone dress up as a ghost to scare us away."

"A ghost?" Mr. Snyder chuckled. Ignoring Marvin, he spoke to Detective Farrow. "Children today have such imaginations. It must come from watching too much television."

"I think I believe these children," said Uncle Ned.

Mr. Snyder's eyes narrowed. "I doubt *anyone* would take the word of these children over mine."

"It may not have to be just our word," Marvin said. "For instance, Mrs. Muncie at the library told us about someone who was very interested in the ghost of Liberty Corners. She described you very well."

"That proves nothing, young man," Mr. Snyder snarled. "Lots of people are interested in local history."

"There's only one costume shop in town," Marvin continued. "I looked it up while we were waiting for Detective Farrow. I wonder if they might remember you renting a skeleton costume."

"I didn't rent such a thing," Mr. Snyder said with a smug smile.

"No, I imagine Mr. Klinger did that," Marvin said. He turned to Mr. Klinger, who was still standing next to Mr. Dinkerhoff, his arm around his uncle's shoulders. Before Mr. Klinger could protest, Marvin added quickly, "I wasn't sure until I heard your voice just now. You made a couple of other mistakes, though. Mr. Snyder knew about the finger puppets, even though Mr. Dinkerhoff told us it was a secret."

"I told you my uncle is forgetful," Mr. Klinger answered. "That proves it."

"Maybe," Marvin said. "But why would he tell Mr. Snyder, who wants to see him out of business? And another thing—Mr. Snyder knew that we were camping by the stream. I think he knew because you told him."

"None of this proves anything," Mr. Klinger protested.

Marvin shrugged. "I wondered why Mr. Snyder's car was at the factory so late the other night. He was making plans with you, Mr. Klinger, wasn't he? And if you need any more proof," he said to the investigators, "I suggest you look at those black smudges on Mr. Klinger's hands. I think you will find they match the goo on the spigot of the barrel. I think you will find the same black goo on the hand Mr. Snyder is hiding in his pocket, and perhaps even some rather good fingerprints on the spigot itself."

"I didn't want to do it," Mr. Klinger whined. "Snyder made me."

Marvin snapped his fingers. "I think Mr. Klinger has been using the factory at night to make some extra money," he said. "That's why Mr. Dinkerhoff mentioned there had been some vandalism. I'll bet supplies were missing, right, Mr. Dinkerhoff?"

Mr. Dinkerhoff nodded. "My nephew told me that kids were breaking into the factory. Or else suggested that I was getting too forgetful to remember what was missing."

"I think Mr. Snyder discovered this somehow. He blackmailed Mr. Klinger into helping him put Mr. Dinkerhoff out of business."

"He saw the lights on in the factory at night. And then he saw me dump some dye

into the creek," Mr. Klinger said to Mr. Dinkerhoff. "But then Snyder said he would report
me if I didn't do it again."

"You weren't all that innocent," snarled
Mr. Snyder. He turned to Detective Farrow.
"As soon as he convinced Mr. Dinkerhoff to
turn over the factory to him, we had a buyer
who wanted to build a motel here. It would
have made us both very rich men."

A uniformed police officer led the two
crooks to the police car and drove away. Uncle
Ned spoke to the environmental investigators.
Then he walked back to the children.

"That was very good," he said.

Marvin looked glum. "I don't think our
parents are going to be impressed," he said.

"Maybe I can put in a good word for you,"
Uncle Ned said, with a wink at Ernie. "Although I have to agree, you took a lot of
unnecessary chances. Next time, come to me
for help, okay?"

"We will," the young detectives agreed.

"I can't believe my own nephew would do
that," said Mr. Dinkerhoff. "I was planning
to retire and leave him the business in a few
more years."

"I guess he didn't want to wait that long,"
Sarah said.

"I didn't know people were so upset about

how the factory looks," Mr. Dinkerhoff said sadly. "I guess it is getting pretty run-down. But I don't have the money to fix it up, and I don't want to put my workers out of a job."

"I've been thinking about that," Kyla said suddenly. "Why don't you sell this property to the people who want to develop the motel? Then use the money to build a new factory near the industrial center."

Mr. Dinkerhoff nodded thoughtfully. "It just might work. My nephew was right about one thing. If I do start a new factory, I'm going to have to keep up with the times."

"All I can say about my little buddies," said Ernie as they were walking toward Uncle Ned's car, "is that being with you two is never boring."

"I can hardly wait to see what mystery you'll find next," Kyla said.

Marvin made a face. The others followed his gaze to a car that had just pulled up. Two sets of worried-looking parents were climbing out.

"I think our next mystery may have to wait for a little while," Marvin said.